LUCÍA ASHTA

MAGIC
AWAKENS

THE WITCHING WORLD – BOOK 1

Published by Awaken to Peace Press.

Cover design by Lou Harper.

Edited by Elsa Crites.

ISBN 978-0-9832743-4-6
January 2017

Learn about Lucía's books at LuciaAshta.com.

For Catia,
whose magic is awakening

There are a thousand ways in which magic can cause death.
There are as many in which it can gift true life.

PROLOGUE

I've had to keep a terrible secret for years. Keeping secrets isn't easy or fun, but I've had no choice. The secret is dangerous. The type people kill over.

There have been a few times when I wasn't cautious enough, and I almost revealed it. It's made me realize that I can't keep it to myself any longer. I have to find a way to share the secret, or it will boil over, desperate to get out.

Since I must tell someone, I will tell you. You pose no danger. By the time my words reach you, my body will have faded from this world.

So it is here that I begin, at the beginning of it all, before I knew anything of secrets.

CLAIMING SICKNESS

Father and Mother stood at the entrance of my chamber, minimizing their risk of contagion. They'd forbidden my sisters to be anywhere near the quarantine zone. "What is it, Doctor? What's wrong with her?" Father called from across the room.

Doctor Whittling was the second physician to see me in as many days. The first doctor had no real understanding of what to do with me and left in a hurry, pocketing the payment he'd done little to earn, while murmuring far-fetched hypotheses and generic treatment instructions.

The fidgety Doctor Whittling had no more of an idea of what was wrong with me than the first physician but truly wished to see me recover. With meaty fingers, he brushed aside strands of red hair, plastered against my forehead, saturated with sweat and dark as blood in the dim light.

Mother ordered the servants to change my soaked bed linens just before sunset, but it made no difference. The fever was strong. The fresh sheets clung to my slick skin.

Doctor Whittling lifted my eyelids with gentle fingers and drew a candle near to examine my clouded eyes. Before shifting his gaze to my parents, he let out a heavy sigh of resignation. The round little doctor froze, knowing he couldn't retract it, while everyone in the room pretended to ignore his lament and what it implied.

"I'm uncertain of the cause of her affliction, nor do I know why it settled into her body so rapidly, but I can say that her condition is very dangerous. Unless her fever breaks shortly, you may lose her."

Doctor Whittling looked toward the doorway with a practiced expression of regret. He delivered this kind of news regularly. It was an unavoidable part of his profession.

Unlike the physicians and my parents, I knew what had caused my illness. Over the last several feverish days, between hallucinations, I realized that I'd claimed it. I told my mother, "I am sick." And so I'd become.

I'd never had a thought like that before, and now I wonder if the feverish hallucinations were what allowed me to reach through to what had not yet come.

But first, I had to survive, and the fever had a vise-like grip on me, fragile and devastated as I was.

A DREADED GRAND ARRIVAL

*I*t all began on a particularly cold day. Nestled in the countryside, Norland was a beautiful place, but during the winter months, a bone-chilling, damp cold was the price to pay for the future reward of sunshine and verdant landscapes.

I woke to the subdued sounds of my lady's maid stoking the fire. Her trembling silhouette clinched her shawl closer around her neck and shoulders. Her body relaxed only when the fire stretched from the night's sleep and awakened.

"Good morning, Maggie," I said.

She turned, surprised. "Good day, Milady. I'm sorry to have disturbed you. I didn't mean to."

"It's all right. I was ready to waken. Has day broken yet?"

"Only just, Milady."

It wasn't possible to open the shutters and let in the morning light. It was too cold early in the day at this time of year, nearing the winter solstice. Maggie opened the shutters only during the height of the day, and even then, for only an hour or two at most.

She scuttled around the room lighting the candles left from the previous evening. She looked much older than her years, still hunched with the memory of an overbearing cold. She was only as old as I was.

"Shall I prepare your clothes, Milady?"

I stretched. My bed was warm. I was reluctant to leave it. I knew how cold the stone floors were.

"I suppose so. I think I'll wear my green dress, the thick one."

Maggie was already assembling the small pile of clothing expected of a future countess. "Perhaps Milady may want to reconsider. Today the Count and Countess of Chester are arriving. Perchance your new violet dress would be a better choice."

I groaned. The violet dress was not as warm, and the sleeves and bodice were tight and itchy. But Maggie knew better than I did what my parents expected of me. I'd learned long ago that resistance to her suggestions was futile. Inevitably, my mother would send me back to dress precisely as Maggie had recommended in the first place.

"Maggie, I wish you looked like me. Then you could take my place, and I'd be free to do as I wish."

Maggie laughed aloud. Behind closed doors, we could be friends. Outside of them, my mother wouldn't allow it. "There's no one that would mistake us for the other."

She was right. In most ways, we were polar opposites. With her dark, straight hair and stocky body, there was no confusing us.

"Besides, I'm not sure I'd want to trade places with you today, Milady."

I searched her eyes. The orange of the fire played across her face in a game of shadows and light but revealed nothing.

"The Count is in a serious mood this morning." Even though we were close, Maggie still wouldn't cross certain boundaries. She was always careful, and I wondered what that was like, always monitoring what she said. I suppose I was the same in a way. My circumstances didn't allow me to be myself either.

Maggie looked away, pretending to be distracted by the choice in shoes to match my outfit. But she didn't fool me. She'd grown up in the castle, shadowing her mother, who shadowed my mother as her lady's maid. Maggie had heard my mother's commands, complaints, and impossible requests in the place of nursery rhymes. She'd learned the punctilious requirements of a life of nobility from a master.

"The Count and Countess of Chester are bringing their son."

I didn't say anything. We both knew what that meant.

My parents were trying to marry me. They'd been searching for a suitable match for some time. I wondered what this latest arrangement offered the Court of Norland.

I closed my eyes and rolled over in bed, trying to block out my life. "I think I was born into the wrong family." Goose down filling muffled my voice, but Maggie interpreted my mumbles. I'd made the same statement to her many times before.

"Our lives are in the hands of God, Milady. I don't think He makes mistakes."

I'd heard that same answer many times before too.

It didn't make me feel any better.

~

I sat in front of the mirror that had once been my mother's. Its carved wooden frame was busy with leaves and flowers. I watched Maggie painstakingly braid my hair, mostly in silence. She was aware of what I was thinking and left me to my thoughts—What would this son of the House of Chester be like? Would my parents force me to marry him even if I didn't like him?

Maggie twirled the finished braids and pinned them into place atop my head. Even if she hadn't already announced it, I would have known: Today I was to look my best. She reserved the pins adorned with freshwater pearls for special occasions.

Maggie picked out two auburn strands to either side of my face and encouraged their natural curl. Then she surveyed me, satisfied with her work. "Now make sure not to move around too much so your hair doesn't fall out."

She was perpetually dismayed at how my hair tumbled out of the intricate hairdos she put me in. I met Maggie's gaze in the mirror. "I'll do my best." Both she and I knew I only partly meant what I said.

I stood so Maggie could tighten my corset further.

"Breathe in," she said.

"I hope this one breath will last me until dark. You know I can't breathe in this thing."

"It's the price you pay for beauty."

It was a hollow statement. My beauty was more evident when I was free of all this artifice.

Maggie smiled a sympathetic smile and handed me pearl drop earrings. "There. Pretty as a picture you are, Milady."

I looked in the mirror at a girl who was beginning to resemble the striking woman she would become. Still, all I saw was emptiness reflected in eyes that looked like someone else's instead of mine. A weak smile at Maggie did nothing to bring life to my naturally sparkling amber eyes.

I turned and made my way down the hall. This being such an important day for them, Father and Mother would be waiting for me to begin breakfast. Maggie helped me with the ample skirts of my dress down the wide stairs from the family rooms of the second floor to the entry hall. She wished me luck before leaving me to walk the hall to the dining room by myself. When I took my seat at the table, I was the last to arrive, even though the sun was still low in the sky.

"Good morning, darling," Mother said with a pleasant-looking smile while she looked me over approvingly. My five sisters and I watched her. "Did you rest well?" This mother was much less business-like than what we were accustomed to.

"Yes, Mother, I did. Thank you."

"Today, the Count and Countess of Chester will be visiting us," my father said in his usual straight-to-it style. "They are bringing their son."

He paused to sip his tea. He let his words hang densely above the chestnut dining table. Then he made measured eye contact with each of us. He began with my youngest sister. Gertrude was eleven, but she knew as well as any of us what the look meant. He ended with me. I was the one he was most worried about.

"You will all be on your very best behavior while the Count and Countess are here." There was no need for Father to mention the consequences if we were to misbehave. We all knew the repercussions would be severe.

"This is important to our family, and we will put the well-being of our family first." Although he spoke to all of us, this statement was directed only at me. My parents expected me to put their well-being before my own happiness. This was my duty in life, and it would also be the fate shared by my sisters.

My siblings looked back at Father with obedient blue eyes. They accepted what he told them without question. Only Gertrude showed signs of a rebellious spirit in a flash of honey eyes that were very much like mine.

Of my four sisters, only Gertrude looked like me. The spark of our inner fire revealed itself in our copper hair color. Our other sisters had blonde, straight hair, as if not even their hair considered deviating from the norm.

"Yes, Father," I said. I was the only one who needed to reply.

"Good." He leaned back in his chair. The solid, dark wood accepted his large frame stoically. "They'll be arriving soon. Break your fast so you can be ready to welcome them."

The rest of the meal was devoid of the usual chatter that followed my sisters everywhere they went. They restrained their easy-going manner in the presence of our parents.

On normal days, we were left to the care of governesses and ladies' maids, while Father and Mother tended to matters of the estate—that seemed often to involve the attendance of hunting and tea parties and dinners that extended late into the night.

"Excuse me, Milord," interrupted the butler. "Little William has spotted the Count and Countess of Chester at the bottom of the drive. They will arrive shortly."

Father pushed his chair back. "Thank you, Henry."

As we each stood, Father and Mother examined us. We passed inspection, all of us in our finest dresses and ornate coiffure.

"Gertrude, remove that jam from your upper lip," Mother snapped. She then plastered what would pass as a joyful smile on her face and took Father's extended arm. They began to make their way to the entry hall.

Even as we were leaving the dining room, Bertha and John were hastily removing any traces of our unfinished breakfast. Everything had to be in order for the grand arrival.

Three blonde heads fell into step behind Father and Mother, but Gertrude came to my side and took my hand. I squeezed hers, anticipating the introduction to my potential future husband. We joined the procession together, dread weighing down our steps.

TREPIDATION BLESSED BY HOPEFUL COLORS

*T*he clop of hooves and wheels dragging behind them on the cobblestone drive finally came to a stop in front of the manor. The footsteps of a horseman and footman descended on the pavement. The men would soon begin to open doors for the passengers.

I couldn't see anyone. Father and Mother decided that the appropriate place for us to receive our guests was in the entry hall, not outside. So all Gertrude and I could make out was the wide stone steps that connected entrance and drive.

The sound of a tired horse nickering wafted into the entryway, and my stomach tied into a big, unpleasant knot.

Henry appeared at the threshold of the massive wooden paneled door: "The Count and Countess of Chester." Then he stepped aside to allow them entry.

The Counts of Chester and Norland shook hands then circled around each other in a practiced move of the nobility to kiss the extended hands of each other's wives.

The Countesses curtsied to each other with trained faultless smiles.

"Heir to the Count and Countess of Chester," Henry said, and all six daughters looked up as I caught the first glimpse of my suitor.

He looked as nervous as I did, trailing behind his parents. He locked eyes with me. As the oldest, I was the tallest and easy to spot. His mouth turned up slightly in tentative entreaty, and I felt the knot in my stomach loosen a notch.

Gertrude squeezed my hand discreetly. She, too, was relieved. He looked nice, although it was still unfathomable to comprehend that this boy might soon become my husband.

The relief in my stomach was short-lived. The servants approached the doorway with two large trunks. It was too much luggage for a day's visit. I sensed my sisters suppressing the same groan I did. Our parents would of course extend the invitation for as long as the guests wanted to stay.

It was going to be a very long day.

～

"It really is too bad that you have so many daughters," the Countess of Chester said in a pause between bites at dinner. The candlelight flickered across her face in sinister slashes and waves. "Not a son among them all."

"Charles contracted small pox when he was only four.

His death has been our cross to bear," said Mother.

"What a shame." The Countess of Chester looked us over unconcernedly. "At least they're all pretty. That should make it easier to find suitable matches for them. We're fortunate to have had two boys. Male heirs are always best."

I cringed inside but was careful to keep my visible expression acceptable. I'd been mindful of Father's warning all day.

"Samuel is a good son. He will marry whomever we think is best for him. Isn't that right, Samuel?"

"Yes, Mother." I sympathized with what I imagined was Samuel's restrained misery. We'd gotten along well so far but surely no one wanted to marry a stranger.

"That's how it should be," Father said. "I'm sure that's what we all did, in our generation. We didn't question our parents' judgment. And now we see that our parents did know best."

The adults nodded in agreement and muttered some comments about how today's children were so much more rebellious than they'd ever thought of being.

I resisted my tongue's impulse to unravel and strike with words like a viper. Rebellious? How might we be rebellious when our parents told us what we must do every important step of the way? Their comments were ridiculous.

I flicked my gaze to Samuel and wondered if he shared any of my thoughts. If he did, I couldn't tell from his immutable expression. He played the role of the consummate son of a count and countess well.

My mind glazed over even as the adults discussed the possibility of my marriage to Samuel. I made a mental note to check the atlas later to find the exact location of Chester. I risked a look at Gertrude and found her looking at me already. I bore a tear back, and Gertrude turned her gaze to her food. She'd barely eaten, even though I knew Martha's crêpes were one of her favorite dishes.

Bertha and John cleared the last of the pear compote, cheeses, and nuts.

"Children, you will go to the playroom with your governesses." Father's eyes rested on me, but he addressed Samuel. "Samuel, would you like to join Clara in the library?" That was the moment I realized I ceased to be a child in Father and Mother's eyes.

Now, I was a business transaction.

"Yes, Sir," Samuel said.

"It would be good for you two to acquaint yourselves. And you will, of course, be chaperoned." Father turned to the staff. "John, let Maggie know she's needed in the library."

"Right away, Milord."

"Let's retire somewhere more private," the Count of Chester said to Father. "We have much to settle."

Father pushed back his chair. "What's your liking? Brandy? Cognac?"

"Good man," the Count of Chester said. "Those will work for me."

Father made eye contact with Bertha. She nodded and retreated to the kitchen. She knew the drill.

The women would not be part of the business talk. After a lifetime of it, they knew their places well, and they withdrew to the fireside in Mother's favorite parlor.

Awkwardly, Samuel and I advanced to the library. I was acutely aware of every step he took and how his body moved close to mine as we walked. We collided more than once. By the time we made it to the library, embarrassment flushed our faces, and I wished the night would just be over already.

Maggie waited for us while she tended a burgeoning fire, and I flashed her a grateful look. I was glad it was she and no one else that would witness this uncomfortable exchange.

~

That first night, Samuel and I performed a stilted routine of empty pleasantries. But by the second day, our parents left us alone while they went on hunts and picnics, and Samuel and I discovered that we enjoyed each other's company.

Of course, what we appreciated most was not on our parents' imagined list of ladylike and gentlemanly activities. However, they didn't know exactly what we did, just that we were appropriately supervised by a lady's maid.

Samuel and I ran through the gardens behind the house when the sun was brightest, dispelling the chill of winter and leaving Maggie far behind. As was her obligation as my lady's maid, assigned to supervise courtship, she went through the motions of monitoring us at all times. However, her motions were purposefully half-hearted.

If anyone at the manor house understood my predicament, it was she. She was working hard to conceal her compassion from Samuel, but I saw it. I'd never been more grateful that Maggie had Mother's trust.

"You know," Samuel said, "I'd been dreading coming here to meet you."

I laughed, and he continued. "Since the very moment my parents announced that I was to marry the 'eldest daughter of the House of Norland. Quite a catch,' they said. 'And pretty too.'" He blushed, but only for a second.

"I'd been dreading meeting you too," I said. "It's such a strange thing, isn't it? To think that our parents arrange for us to marry with no thought as to whether or not we'll get along or even like each other."

I paused to look at the sandy blonde hair that had broken loose of the careful haircut meant to keep every strand of hair in place. It fell across Samuel's forehead, making him look more like a boy than a young man.

"What could be more important than the person you share your life with? Yet for our parents, it's all about wealth and power, and a deal that benefits both parties."

It was a bold thing to say. I'd barely met Samuel, and I was a girl. Girls weren't supposed to voice their opinions unless they were restricted to fashion and needlepoint.

Yet, Samuel seemed to appreciate my opinion. A dash of hope dared to skip across my frightened heart.

"I fully agree. I've been hearing about what my future wife would need to bring to the table in order for us to marry for so long now that it seems that my parents have completely forgotten that I'm a person not a bargaining chip, and that my future wife is too." His glance toward me was cautious.

"Do you know what your parents are getting out of our marriage?" I didn't dare look at Samuel after I asked. I was certain this was crossing the boundaries of what a bride was allowed to say. But I had to ask. My future happiness was being dealt away. At the very least, I wanted to know why.

"Oh, I think Father is getting a summer house in Wilkershire out of it along with a substantial dowry. Maybe some horses too. I don't know precisely. I haven't exactly been part of the negotiations."

Wow. The summer house in Wilkershire. It was a large house that Mother had worked hard to get just right. We went there for weeks at a time during the summers, and Mother worked almost non-stop on the interior décor and the maintenance of the gardens while we were there.

"The house in Wilkershire is a working estate," I said. "Lots of farmsteads."

Samuel shrugged noncommittally.

A minute passed in silence while I gathered the courage to ask what I wanted to next. I nibbled on the inside of my lip. We watched some birds pecking at the ground, searching for food. "Do you know what my parents are receiving in exchange for our union?"

"I do." Even though I wasn't yet familiar with Samuel's ways, it sounded like he was trying to keep aversion from his voice. "Father has entered the King's favor as of late. The King has already promised him a new title. The Duke of Luchesy opposed the King's new taxation policies, and so the King is stripping him of his title and his lands."

"I see." And I did. That meant that the Count of Chester would soon become the Duke of Luchesy. If Samuel was in line to become a duke, then as his wife, I would be in line to become a duchess. Father and Mother dreamt of being the parents of a duchess.

"My parents are selling me off for land and wealth. Your parents are selling you off for a title and the King's favor." He laughed a bitter laugh. It was in that instant that I decided I liked him—or, at least, that I would learn to like him. Neither one of us appreciated what our parents were doing to us, nor did he seem to appreciate the cutthroat tactics of the nobility.

He turned toward me. The sun filtered between distant tree branches to freckle his face with light. "The pairing could have been worse though. Right?"

His smile was a timid entreaty. "I think we could learn to like each other, regardless of titles and obligations." Even though he didn't pose this last part as a question, it was one. Would I be willing to give our union a real chance and make the best of a difficult situation?

He waited for an answer, tension creeping back into his limbs the longer I took to reply.

Finally, I smiled. "Of course. We can find a way to make this work. As you say, it could have been worse. Much worse."

"You have no idea. My parents tried to arrange marriages with other girls before you. All the alliances fell through. Thank God. I met the girl that was to be my fiancée in the most recent marriage negotiations."

"What was she like?"

"Oh she was terrible. Well, perhaps not terrible, but I was terrified at the thought of a life with her."

"Why?" Unlike most young ladies in my position, I didn't enjoy gossip. Still, I couldn't resist my curiosity.

"All she spoke of was the latest fashion, her hair, her makeup, and the silly comings and goings of those in our social circle. When my parents took me to meet her, she spent an entire half-day speaking of a scandalous affair at the King's court. I thought I would die from boredom and acute lack of interest right then."

I smiled, this time a genuine one. He smiled back, mimicking my warmth.

"Why did your parents reject her, and the other prospects, as your bride?" I asked, although perhaps the answer was an obvious one.

Samuel shrugged. "I think it had much to do with your father making mine the better offer. Now it will probably be my brother's fate to marry that girl. As soon as Father marries me off, he'll be onto Winston next."

"Oh, poor Winston then. If this girl is as trivial as you say she is."

Samuel tensed, inexplicably, I thought. "Yes, well, Winston can take care of himself. I'd worry more about the girl than him. I'll pity whichever unfortunate girl ends up marrying my brother."

I turned to him, amber eyes alive with inquisitiveness. I didn't connect much with three of my sisters, the middle ones, but I liked them even though we were different from each other. Samuel didn't sound as if he liked Winston at all.

Samuel shrugged again in answer to my unspoken question. "He's unkind," he said, then looked away, beyond the manicured shrubbery of the gardens, gazing at memories of other times. "He's always been quite purposefully cruel to me and our younger sisters. Even when he was a boy. I'm two years older than him, but he's the bully in the family. He's always had this mean streak in him. He enjoys causing others pain."

There was a long pause while I considered how fortunate I was to have the five sisters I did. Sure, we fought just like any siblings did. But none of my sisters had ever done anything to hurt me on purpose.

Samuel visibly reined himself in from unpleasant recollections. "Thankfully, Winston has nothing to do with our alliance. And I'll have no interest in continuing any kind of relationship with him once we're married. If we're lucky, once you meet him at the wedding, neither one of us will ever have to see him again."

I nodded, not knowing what else to do in response to this terrible brother I hadn't heard of until just then.

Samuel grew silent again for another minute, and when he continued speaking, he was wistful. "I'd given up on thinking that my future wife might be someone whose company I'd enjoy."

"You're the first of my potential suitors that I've met."

"Let's hope I'm also the last." He reached a hand toward mine, snuck a glance behind his shoulder—no sign of Maggie catching up to us—and squeezed and held my hand in his. "I think that we may enjoy a life together." A pause while he searched my eyes. "Do you?"

With the sun hitting them, his eyes were the color of Father's favorite brandy. "I do."

Samuel grinned. "Good. Then that's settled."

It was a futile attempt at reclaiming a bit of the power our parents had taken from us. We were going through motions that would have no effect on our parents' negotiations, but it still felt nice to think we had some choice in the matter that would determine so much of our future.

Samuel bounced up from the bench we sat on, pulling me up with him. "Now, why don't you show me a bit more of the gardens before your lady's maid finds us?"

He led me by the hand into the hedge-trimmed labyrinth. I followed, giggling. We were two children at play, locked into the roles of adults by our parents.

We separated in the labyrinth, hiding from each other, tumbling into shrubbery and losing our way, and then finally laughing until our sides hurt when we discovered each other. Our cheeks flushed pink as much from excitement as from the cold.

In the late afternoon, we took a carriage ride through the countryside, bundled in blankets. We ignored the scenery as Samuel told stories of his childhood, and I relished the adventures only boys were allowed to have.

"Don't worry," Samuel had promised, "once we marry, I'll teach you how to fish. We can slip away without telling anyone where we're going. When we are lord and lady of our own house, we won't have to give any explanations about anything. We can spend our days fishing if we want to."

"Really? That sounds fabulous. Mother never lets my sisters or me do anything fun. We're only allowed to do 'ladylike' things. And I've discovered that ladylike activities are rarely fun."

"We can spend our days fishing and traipsing through the mud if you desire it." Mischief flashed across his face, and I realized it was unlikely that he'd been allowed to traipse through the mud much either. If his parents were anything like other counts and countesses I'd met, children were meant to be kept mostly out of sight and always impeccably proper and clean.

Samuel instructed the driver to pull over by a small pond. We fed ducks some bread Samuel had stashed in his pocket with the hope of finding exactly these interested parties. When the bread ran out, Samuel took my hand, and we ran away from the ducks together.

The ducks followed us all the way up the hill to the carriage before they relented, which was a good thing, because neither Samuel nor I could stand straight from so much laughter. We would have been easy pickings for a belligerent duck.

Even Maggie, sitting next to the driver up front, had a smile on her face as Samuel helped me back onto my seat. When the driver turned the horses back toward Norland, the sun began to set, coloring the sky and my heart with hopeful colors.

When Father sent Samuel and me to the library again that night, we didn't sit on different armchairs as we had the night before. We shared a loveseat, though we sat at an appropriate distance from each other under Maggie's supervision—with the knowledge that a parent could walk into the library at any time.

We settled comfortably into the stuffed upholstery and the knowing that good fortune had finally shone upon us.

Our parents would obligate us to marry, but we would enjoy pleasant companionship and a chance at a good life together.

When the guests' carriage pulled away the next morning, Samuel waved to me out the window. I watched the carriage long after Father and Mother had gone in, until Samuel's face became a speck in the distance and I could no longer see his smile. Then the horses turned at the end of our long drive and pointed toward Chester.

THE UNHAPPY HAPPY NEWS

I'd grown used to the idea: Samuel and I would marry in springtime. Mother and the Countess of Chester were consumed with the punctilious details of a wedding celebration worthy of our status, exchanging almost daily correspondence with an urgency I didn't share.

My life hadn't changed at all in the present. My days were occupied with the usual lessons—geography, literature, Latin, French, Italian, and piano—under the tutelage of our demanding governesses. My sisters and I were escorted outside for fresh air in the afternoons, allowed to remain in the gardens for longer than before now that the days were beginning to warm up. Spring was just around the corner.

In the evenings, our governesses led us through interests appropriate to young women with the destinies we all shared thanks to our birth: to become good wives of the nobility. We embroidered flowers on all sorts of doilies while our governesses reminded us that we should learn to find fulfillment in these kinds of things.

But even as my life hadn't changed in the immediate, the idea of my future loomed above me with all the threat of dark and foreboding clouds, harbingers of a violent thunderstorm. As much as I liked Samuel and was at ease knowing I'd escaped a much worse fate with a much worse groom, there was no denying the nearly-constant jumble of nerves in my stomach.

My life was about to become nearly unrecognizable.

Our entire family would travel to Chester. I would marry, and only my parents and sisters would return to Norland Manor. I'd remain behind to begin a life with my new husband. I would be under the tutelage of my mother-in-law, and she would teach me the duties of the wife of a potential future count and duke.

I had no more of a say in the planning of my future than I did of my present or my past. However, I'd managed one small victory. Although to Mother it was next to nothing, a decision she made quickly for reasons entirely free of emotion, it meant the world to me.

Maggie and I had gone over how I would say it dozens of times. I practiced precisely what I would say and precisely how I would say it. However, as I prepared to knock on the open door to the study where Mother was bent over her desk writing the Countess of Chester, my nerves wouldn't settle. All of a sudden, my collar felt too tight, my corset unbearably oppressive, and my palms sweaty.

I knocked. Without looking over her shoulder, Mother told me to wait a minute. That minute expanded into at least thirty in my mind before Mother gave me her full attention and gestured for me to take a seat next to her.

"What is it, Clara?"

"Well, Mother, I, um, was hoping to speak with you about something."

"How many times do I have to tell you, Clara? 'Um' is so unladylike. Omit it from your speech."

"Yes, Mother."

She cast a regretful glance at the correspondence I interrupted before sitting back in the high seat of her chair and folding her hands across her lap.

Her eyes were fixed on me. A rivulet of sweat began to snake its way along the bones of my corset.

"I was thinking, perhaps it would be a good idea for Maggie to accompany me once I settle at the Court in Chester."

Mother arched her eyebrows. I hurried on. "Maggie knows so much about the ways of the nobility, having been guided by her mother, your own lady's maid, who learned it all from you. Maggie would help me with how I should dress and behave once I marry Samuel. She would make sure that I adjust to the Court there well."

Mother's face was immutable.

"I trust Maggie to always guide me in a way that supports my best. And the family's, of course."

Something crossed Mother's eyes then, and I secretly commended myself for thinking to add the point about Maggie being able to guide me toward the well-being of my parents whom I represented even after I married. Maggie and I hadn't discussed my saying this in all our rehearsals.

But of course it would all come down to this. How did my actions and choices benefit Mother and Father? Wasn't that what all my life had been about?

"Perhaps you have a good point, Clara," Mother said, as if that was unexpected. "The ways of the court and the nobility have never mattered enough to you. It's as if you have no idea how fortunate you are to lead the life of a lady.

"Having Maggie there with you can only help. You'll need to be very careful to do exactly what is expected of you as Samuel's wife. It's imperative that everyone at Court accept you so that your transition into your future life and its titles will be guaranteed."

Mother studied me, and I did my best not to wonder what she saw as her eyes swept me up and down. "Yes, Maggie will go with you to Chester."

She turned her attention back to her letter. "Shouldn't you be studying right now, Clara?" she said to her desk.

I retreated from the study, confused. I'd achieved the small victory I set out to accomplish, yet I didn't feel victorious. Around Mother, I never did.

Maggie would have to leave her mother and everything familiar to her behind, but she thought the change of scenery might be good. She'd never ventured far from Norland.

"Perhaps I'll meet a boy there that likes me, and he and I will marry." She and I were behind the closed doors of my chambers, where Maggie became a different person. "Wouldn't that be amazing, Milady?"

I didn't think marriage was much to look forward to, but Maggie saw it as an escape from a life spent attending to others. It made me sad, and I wished I could do more for her than share encouragement I didn't believe in.

"I will be very happy for you to meet a boy you can love and marry." I mentioned love; she hadn't. She considered me a romantic for thinking love played any part in marriage. But what kind of life would it be if it were devoid of love? "And I do hope you meet him at the Court in Chester. It will be so very nice to have a friend there. I'll miss home terribly, especially Gertrude."

I was trying not to think too much about what it would be like to leave my favorite little sister behind. Just remembering that I only had a few more weeks to share with her made me anxious.

Of course, I would miss my other sisters too, but Gertrude and I shared something that we didn't with the others. She and I were similar. We yearned for excitement in life. We found beauty and intrigue in that which our sisters did not.

Gertrude and I had spent countless hours together— when our governesses deemed it appropriate—in the garden and lakeside. We examined plants and animals with an enthrallment our sisters didn't understand.

"I think I'll like to stay at the court in Chester, Milady. Chester sounds interesting, and I've never gone from home before." Maggie's eyes were dreamy. I envied that she could look forward to what I dreaded.

Even knowing that Samuel was a nice boy didn't make it much easier to leave the only home I'd ever known and the sister I loved more than anyone else.

"I wonder what he'll be like," Maggie said in a wistful voice I didn't hear often.

"Who?"

"The boy I'll marry, silly! I mean, Milady."

I smiled softly. I'd asked Maggie to stop calling me "milady" while in my chambers many times, but she insisted. She feared that she might get overly used to it and address me improperly in public. I didn't like the formality between us, but I couldn't blame her. Mother dealt with impropriety harshly, and I didn't wish her attention on Maggie.

"Well, he'll be handsome, of course," I indulged her. "He'll be kind and fun. And he'll have lines that crinkle around his eyes from so much laughter and sunshine."

"Yes! He'll be all of that!"

"And he'll like to kiss you under the moonlight," I teased, but Maggie loved it. Her wistful eyes grew rounder, and she was lost to her dreaming.

Then there was a knock at the door.

Maggie jumped up from her usual seat next to the hearth, straightened her uniform, and opened the door with her composure properly in place.

The woman on the other side of the door looked very much like Maggie, although age had softened her features. Years of service had taught her to accept her life as it was and to find joy wherever she could.

"Hello Margaret," she said with a smile.

"Hello Mum."

"The Countess would like to see Lady Clara as soon as possible."

Maggie nodded. "Yes, Mother. I'll tell her now."

The woman's kind eyes clouded over. "There has been news from the Court at Chester."

~

"*M*other? You called for me?" I stood at the entrance to her chambers.

"Yes, Clara. Come in.

"Take a seat. Warm yourself by the fire."

Mother searched my eyes. Had I heard the news already? "We received a missive from Chester this morning."

A flutter of hope rose within me. Maybe it was a letter from Samuel for me.

"There has been a change in circumstances with the Count's eldest son, Samuel."

Hope forgotten, I waited for it. I struggled to keep my body from shaking with nerves and emotion. I knew my parents' ways too well.

Mother turned to look out the window as she continued. "One of Samuel's earlier prospects has unexpectedly come into wealth and the Count and Countess of Chester find themselves obligated to entertain a new offer the girl's family has made them. The family is able to offer the House of Chester substantially more than we are."

Mother grimaced but moved on quickly, with the resilience of a good noblewoman, prepared to make the best of any situation, finding the advantage to any disadvantage.

"We can't truly blame the Count and Countess of Chester as your father and I would have done the same if this had happened to us. It's the smart thing to do. And since there was no written contract between us outlining the terms of the marriage, we have no recourse to hold against Chester.

"However, the Count of Chester has generously offered that you marry his second son. While this second son, Winston, isn't set up to inherit the title of count nor potentially that of duke, there's always the chance that Samuel will die and Winston will inherit after all.

"Also, the Count of Chester has softened the blow for us by offering the title of Earl of Lombarge to Winston. One of the Count's relatives is about to pass without inheritors, and the title will pass on to him. The Count of Chester has agreed to enter into a written agreement that will reserve the title of earl for Winston. Hence, you will become an earl's wife.

"Of course, your father and I find ourselves forced to accept this alternate arrangement and have already responded with our acceptance to the Count of Chester's proposal, before he has the chance to change his mind. This time, we'll be sure to secure a written contract immediately. You'll still marry in the spring, and everything will continue as arranged."

No. Nothing would continue as planned. Nothing was as it had been moments before. It was enough to come to terms with marrying one stranger, but it was quite another to dismiss the boy I'd come to like for yet another stranger, one that I almost certainly wouldn't like at all.

From Samuel's description of his brother, it seemed rather likely that my marriage to Winston would be a very unhappy one in which I would be subject to his constant mistreatment. Samuel had made it clear: Winston was a cruel person who enjoyed making others suffer.

Mother turned to look at me, as if she finally remembered that this concerned me. Her blue eyes were piercing. "Will there be any problems?"

What was I to say to that? My life felt like one big problem after another.

"Clara. Will there be any problems?"

I couldn't meet her eyes as I answered: "No, Mother. May I be excused now?" I couldn't bear to be in her presence a moment longer.

"Yes, you may. I'll tell your father the happy news."

As I left the room, I wondered how she could possibly say that after seeing my reaction. But then, she and I were nothing alike.

I had only one thought: to find Gertrude. I wished we could run away together and never come back.

THE GAPING VOID OF THE FUTURE

*T*hat same afternoon, a letter arrived, but my parents didn't find out about it. The letter was from Samuel. He'd given it to an envoy with instructions to entrust the letter only to Maggie from Norland Manor's staff. The messenger had followed his master's instructions explicitly and, with a little luck, he'd arrived at a time when the Count and Countess of Norland were away.

Maggie's mother had been standing in the entryway when the horseman arrived but agreed to keep the confidence. Still, despite the fortune that surrounded the delivery of Samuel's letter, it didn't extend to its contents. Maggie left me alone to read it, and when she came back, she found me crying on the bed, desolate.

"What's the matter, Milady?"

I was unable to answer her.

Apprehensively, she picked up the letter from the bed quilt.

*D*earest Clara,

    It is with great regret that I write you this letter. By now, you have certainly learned of the change in our fate. We will not marry in spring. In my stead, you will marry my brother.

    This news saddens my heart deeply, not only because I have learned to care for you and to look forward to the life we would share together, but also because of who my brother is. I would not wish him as a husband upon my enemy. It pains me that you will have to endure the suffering that will undoubtedly come from being his wife.

    As we have no decision in this matter, I relegate to prayer that this will change. I pray for a miraculous intervention that will set things right and allow you and I to unite.

    I am ever so sorry, dearest Clara, and I hope that you will keep a place in your heart for me, no matter what the circumstances. You have a spot in mine that no one can replace.

    Eternally yours,

    Samuel

"*O*h no, Clara. I'm so very sorry." Maggie forgot all about propriety. She sat on the bed next to me and placed her hand on my back while I sobbed.

The moments passed, long and drawn out, yet I couldn't stop crying.

I tried to move on from the anguish. I tried to pull myself out of it, but it had swallowed me whole.

I didn't notice when Maggie got up and left the room. I still didn't notice when she returned with Gertrude. As soon as Gertrude read the letter, she flung herself on the bed next to me and cried too.

When her tears passed, she pulled herself close to me and held me, and I couldn't remember ever being more grateful for my sister. She remained with me in her arms until Maggie came to retrieve us for dinner.

~

"I can't possibly come down to dinner. You'll have to tell Mother that I'm ill."

Maggie looked at me, still crumpled across the bed. "I understand, Milady, but you know how much the Countess dislikes it when you don't dine with her." I could already hear Mother's words: A proper family should have a proper dinner.

"Are you certain that's what you want me to tell her, Milady?"

"I'm certain."

Not even five minutes later, Mother came to my chambers. "What's the meaning of this, Clara? Are you truly sick? You looked well enough this morning."

"I am sick. I can't come down for dinner."

"Nonsense. You're just throwing a fit. Gertrude, go down to dinner immediately."

Gertrude was a strong-willed eleven-year-old, but I didn't blame her for cowering at Mother's harsh tone. She slid off the bed, leaving Mother and me alone.

"Clara, you will go to dinner right now."

I always obeyed or, at least, I was mindful to give the

appearance of obedience. But today had been too much. In that moment, I couldn't obligate myself to be someone I wasn't—yet again.

I rose on the bed so that I could face Mother. I noticed her startle slightly, although she kept her implacable expression firmly in place.

The anger and sense of injustice I normally kept within boiled up and over. "No, Mother. I will not go down to dinner tonight."

Mother gasped at the insolence. I gathered more courage than I would have thought necessary to continue. "You and Father have doomed me to a life of wretched unhappiness. Winston is a horrible boy, and he will treat me terribly. You've condemned your flesh and blood for selfish reasons, for enough wealth to maintain Norland Manor."

I couldn't be certain how terrible of a boy Winston really was. I was basing all of my impressions of him on Samuel's opinion of his younger brother. However, Samuel and I had connected. We seemed to share a similar view on people. I suspected that I'd find his determination of Winston's personality all too accurate.

Besides, the moment Mother told me Samuel was to marry someone else instead of me, my heart had squeezed in upon itself in anguish, and it still hadn't released its overpowering grip on my emotions. With a heart that felt every one of my crushed hopes at a pleasant life with Samuel, there was no talking reason. I only experienced the vise-like grip of grief and agony.

Ending up with Winston seemed very much like the end of the world. It was the end of my world.

I looked Mother in the eyes, with a blazing fire in my own, and when I spoke, my words could cut through metal. "The least you can do is leave me alone for one night to grieve the loss of my future happiness."

To my great surprise, Mother left the room without response, and I didn't see her again for several days.

Had she not done such a good job of avoiding me, perhaps she might have done something to prevent the illness that overtook me. But by the time she realized how gravely ill I was, there was little anyone could do to help me.

STAY OR LEAVE

"Is there anything we can do to save her, Doctor?" Father asked of Doctor Whittling.

"I'll bleed her to drain the sickness from her body. If we're in luck, I may still draw the illness from her before it completely consumes her. I brought leaches with me, prepared for just such an event. I'll encourage leaches onto her and cut her as well. The faster she bleeds, the better our chances."

This was the beginning of a long litany of experts my parents hired to see me. Doctor Whittling, the second of them, bled me out and weakened me gravely. I came perilously close to dying from his treatment.

Twice, I grasped at elusive alertness as the fever undulated, snake-like, through my consciousness. I glimpsed a moment outside of its hypnotic swirl only for that alertness to notice my spirit wavering within my body.

A single breath, a single thought or gust of wind, could extract me fully from my shell.

But somehow I survived another day, though I don't think it was my strength that did it. The circumstances of life dictated my fate. I didn't choose to stay any more than I chose to leave.

I was an impartial observer. I floated in and out of awareness, each time curious, yet unconcerned, as to what was happening to me. If I died, then I died. My parents had already condemned me to a slow and gradual death as Winston's wife.

The next doctor, a man with a few greasy strands of hair that he kept rearranging across his shiny scalp, made me drink the most horrible tinctures. Even though they made me vomit, he insisted that they would save me, so Mother ordered me to drink them from her place of safety at the threshold. In my still-feverish, frail state, my attempts at resistance accomplished nothing more than exhausting me further.

The fourth and fifth doctors did nothing innovative, but concurred with the previous expert opinions: There was neither much hope nor much time. My parents called the minister to pray over me.

The minister arrived with the sunrise and stayed all day. He left at sunset to rest so he could begin the routine anew the following day. He became a regular fixture at my bedside. His round, middle-aged belly told me he spent much of his time praying over lost causes, and his kindness told me that he believed in what he did.

The Count and Countess of Norland had their legacy to think of. Even as they anticipated my death, they approached no closer than the threshold.

I was relieved they stayed away.

THAT WHICH WAS DORMANT
AWAKENS

It was on one particularly difficult afternoon, in a thick fog that made everything appear illusory, that I considered that I might just go ahead and die that day.

Then a new face showed up at my bedside. It hovered at the periphery of my consciousness like a strong feeling I couldn't shake off.

Dark hair faded into the dark of a cape the man kept wrapped around him despite the heat of a blazing fire. Blue eyes that looked as febrile as my own examined me. His stare was sharp and penetrating. I felt bare, like I couldn't hide anything from him, had I had the will to hide.

But even he, as captivating as he was, faded to the morass of no thought. From that place, I didn't realize what desperation had driven my parents to do.

Throughout the first part of the night, I roused over and again to the sounds of unrecognizable chanting. Then I faded out to the empty space of feverous time.

This dark man and I were alone in my room. He'd banished everyone. If he was to do his work, no one could witness it. Mystery enveloped his ways as tightly as the cloak he still hadn't removed.

In that place of solitude, of desperate vulnerability, a part of me that had long been dormant awakened.

And it would refuse to go back to sleep.

LIFE WITHIN DEATH

I still don't know how many days passed in this way. At some point, one of the servants carried me out to the carriage. Wrapped in blankets, I remember only a burst of cold, crisp air on my face that startled me to temporary alertness. It was air more refreshing than any I could remember; it carried the joy of being alive with it.

I looked into John's concerned face and managed to smile at his kindness. His was the last face I recalled seeing before leaving Norland Manor.

The clop, clop, clop of horse hooves. The uneven rocking of the carriage. Maggie's hand reaching out to feel my clammy forehead. Feeling cold within all my blankets, even while sweat dripped down my sides in unconstrained rivulets.

Maggie coaxing my mouth open to take in a spoonful of water. The occasional snorting of tired horses as they climbed up and down hills. Maggie praying to her God, the one that didn't make mistakes.

Then a soft, cold bed. The bright flames of a new fire, its crackling speaking a language I didn't know. The face of the mysterious man, lifting my eyelids to examine my eyes, the windows to the soul.

And finally, darkness, long and prolonged, free of any thought at all.

Existence within the void of it. Coming alive within death.

I welcomed this death of my old self, and Death eagerly indulged me.

PARTICLES OF MAGIC

I finally awoke. There was no warning. One morning, it was simply all over, and I woke.

I realized I was capable of thought again, and I probed my memory only to soon give up. The gap in it was large and cavernous. It took more energy than I had to explore it.

A trail of sunshine peaked in through partially open shutters. It played with the dust in the air, and I felt inexplicable hope, as if the dust were particles of magic.

The chirps of morning birds found their way through glass, and I realized that I felt different than I had before.

I threw off two top blankets. I was sweating, but no longer from fever. I edged to the side of the bed to swing my feet down, but the effort exhausted me. I propped pillows behind me and sat back instead.

I swooned, darkness clouding the edges of my brain. I closed my eyes to rest from the exertion, the wet cotton of my nightshirt clinging to my breasts, my chest heaving up and down.

I lost time.
I wasn't ready to find it.
Not yet.

A DARK, BROODING MAN

When I opened my eyes next, it was dark outside. Maggie had dozed off in a chair by the fire. The stark firelight exposed the worry and exhaustion in her face.

I watched her sleep, incapable of more than that. I found peace in watching her, in glimpsing a part of life outside myself.

I slid down on the pillows and slept for the rest of the night.

~

It was midday when I next woke. My eyes fluttered open slowly, shuttering away the blur of sleep and the haze of fever past. When they focused, Maggie's smile exploded with brilliance.

"Oh my God, Clara! You're awake!"

Maggie clapped a muted clap and then pressed her smile to her clasped hands. Her eyes watered, and she blinked away tears. "I thought you were going to die, Clara. We all did."

Maggie was breathing irregularly and sniffling. In the midst of my sickness, she'd realized how much we cared about each other. There would be no more "milady" behind closed doors. We were friends.

I tried to smile at her, with poor results.

"No, Clara, don't do anything or try to talk yet. You need to take it really, really slow."

Maggie spooned out water from the pitcher on the bedside table. I drank thirstily. Maggie smiled, accomplished. She'd labored to get me to drink water during my illness, and I would never take in enough. My lips had been perpetually dry and cracking. I felt the discomfort now, for the first time. I drank more water, wincing at the pain in my lips as I moved them.

"Your, uh, doctor is away right now," Maggie said, drawing out the word "doctor" dubiously, and then quickly averting her eyes. I noticed the suspicious behavior, but could do little more. My mind and emotions were already struggling to keep up with the basic conversation.

"He left to get something. He wouldn't say what. He didn't say when he'd be back either, but I don't suppose it'll be long. He never leaves for very long. When he gets back, I can get a message out to your parents. They'll want to know the fever has broken."

Resistance flared in my eyes. I'd forgotten about my impending marriage. Now that I remembered, I didn't want my parents to know I was better—at least not yet. Nothing good would come of it.

Maggie read my expression accurately. "Okay, I won't tell them yet. But I'll have to tell them before long. And what about Gertrude? She's worried sick."

Gertrude. A wave of love and tenderness swept over me. I didn't want her to worry needlessly.

"Shall I send a discrete message to her alone?"

I nodded weakly. That would be perfect, until I decided what I wanted Maggie to say to my parents.

Maggie wrote the note in anticipation of my doctor's arrival. Then, she tended to me. She spoon fed me a warm vegetable broth. I was able to drink only half a cup, but Maggie was satisfied. It was far more than I'd eaten in a very long time.

Under the covers, I could feel my hip bones protruding, my stomach sinking below them. Once I was able to dress again, my clothing would hang loose on me.

I didn't have the strength to bathe submerged in a tub, but Maggie was able to clean me up significantly from where I lay on the bed. I immediately began to feel better. Maggie told me that I had been intensely feverish for a cycle of the moon. That was a very long time to be coated in sweat and out of my mind.

The many experts and doctors who had come to see me had been shocked that my body could survive this long under such duress. They warned my parents that, if by some miracle I survived, I would most likely be feeble minded. No brain could bear such a high fever for long. There would certainly be permanent damage.

My parents had waited to inform the Count and Countess of Chester of my illness for as long as they could, but as the days progressed and morphed into weeks, they sent a messenger to the Court at Chester to warn of the situation.

Winston's parents extended their generosity by offering to delay any decision until a cycle of the moon before the wedding date—they could afford the delay, with their attention focused on the impending nuptials of their eldest, Samuel. If at that time I was still unwell, severely brain damaged, or dead, Winston would marry another. If by then I had recovered or was only mildly brain damaged, the wedding would proceed as arranged. In the meantime, the Count and Countess of Chester would make provisional queries with other families. They would line up a back-up bride for Winston.

Although Maggie had not returned to Norland Manor since we left it, her mother had been sending her letters keeping her abreast of the situation. I was most grateful for the insights and to Maggie's mother for sharing them with us. As my mind regained its usual sharpness, this information would serve me well. It was up to me to carve out a path for my happiness.

For once, I appreciated the misguided opinions of others. The doctors' prognoses provided me with a ripe opportunity for avoiding marital obligation. The wheels in my mind were beginning to break free of the cobwebs, beginning to turn again. I would come up with a plan.

"There he is," Maggie said, interrupting my thoughts.

The sound of a galloping horse drew near, passed right outside the window, and came to a stop not far away.

"Maggie, where are we?" My voice cracked from a throat that had been parched for too long. Maggie had done virtually all of the talking so far.

"You don't recognize this room?"

I looked around. I didn't.

"This is your room. That you share with Gertrude." When Maggie identified the vacuous look on my face, she continued, stating what to her was obvious. "We are at your family's house at Lake Creston."

Lake Creston seemed like a good place to be. It was a day's ride from Norland, which meant I was far from my parents' scrutiny. Besides, I'd always liked our visits to the lake when I was a girl. The visits had grown further apart as I entered adolescence. I hadn't been here in years.

Strong and swift footsteps sounded in the house. In the skip of a heartbeat, the dark, brooding man I vaguely remembered from the haze of fever was at the door. Five long strides put him at bedside. I stared up at him, mesmerized, a little frightened even.

"Maggie, please leave us alone." Even the sound of his voice was different from anything I'd heard before, but I couldn't understand then what made it so.

"Yes, Sir," Maggie said and closed the door behind her.

Who was this man?

I looked up into deep blue, foreboding eyes.

DANGEROUS SECRETS

*H*e examined me very differently than the other doctors. He didn't take my pulse or look at my tongue or in my ears. He did stare into my eyes, but it wasn't to check the dilation of my pupils or the white that surrounded my irises.

His eyes bore into mine. I felt that I shouldn't blink, and I stared back at him—uncomfortable at first, then angry at his encroachment, and finally, indifferent. I settled into myself and released concern over his actions, and it was only then that he seemed satisfied and shifted his gaze.

His eyes scrolled across what was visible of my body. My skin tingled and pricked in heightened awareness everywhere his eyes skimmed. The fine hairs on my arms rose to alertness even though I was warm. His eyes swept the outlines of my waist, hips, legs, and feet beneath the blanket.

I waited. He studied the room, searching for I-don't-know-what. He rose and looked into the fire. He stared at it as intently as he'd stared at me. Then he removed something from his pocket and threw it into the flames.

The fire sparked and sputtered, and as it did, he turned to look at me once more. His gaze was steady although distracted in a way it hadn't been before.

Then he walked out of the room.

I thought he would soon come back, but he didn't. I sat, waiting, until I heard the thundering sounds of a horse leaving the property. Only then did my regular breathing resume. I hadn't even realized I had been holding my breath.

~

I was still too weak to call out for Maggie. I swallowed my impatience as I anticipated her coming to check on me. When she finally did, I spoke even before she reached the bed.

"Maggie, you must tell me all about him. Who is that man? He's unlike any physician I've ever encountered before."

I expected Maggie to smile, perhaps even to blush, and to tell me what she knew of this man my parents had left us alone with.

But she didn't. She looked at me for a moment, turned to look out the window, then looked at me again, a nervousness splaying across her face. She breathed out heavily.

I tensed, anticipating whatever news she had to tell me.

"I've been here at the lake house with him for weeks

waiting for you to wake up. It's only been the two of us in the house. There's a caretaker who tends to the horses and brings us food from the markets, but he stays in a room off the stables. Even though we've been alone in the living quarters all this time, I hardly know anything about him.

"I only know that he's private and secretive. He leaves frequently, always coming back later in the day or by the next, but he never tells me where he's been. He keeps the door to his chambers closed and locked at all times when he's not in them. He speaks little, and even then only says what's necessary.

"I know nothing about him first hand, really. I don't even know his full proper name or where he's from." She looked disappointed, but she was nowhere as disappointed as I felt.

"Surely my parents wouldn't have sent us away with just anyone."

"Your parents were desperate, Clara. Everyone said you'd die. When Martha learned that your parents had given up, that only a minister prayed over you, she asked to see his Lordship, your father. You know that Martha has always loved you, and she was worried about you."

I nodded. Martha had been at Norland Manor since Father was a boy. I'd grown up visiting her in the kitchens whenever I could get away with it. She would bake sweet buns for my sisters and me. I had fond memories of warm hugs among the folds of her skirts.

"She told your father about a—well, about a magician." Maggie tumbled on, avoiding eye contact with me as she did. "She'd heard about this magician when she was in town a few months ago. It was rumored that he'd cured a child in the countryside. The Devil had twisted the boy's legs so that he couldn't walk, and the magician cured him."

Maggie was solemn as she continued, purposefully avoiding my eyes, wide as saucers. "Martha took a big risk telling his Lordship this. But she wanted to see you better."

Martha had taken a big risk indeed. Any association with sorcery was dangerous. The townspeople of Norland and its surrounds were highly superstitious. Rumors sprang like leaks, and no one examined the source of the allegations too closely or too objectively.

Once gossip attributing evil proclivities to a townsperson began, it was nearly impossible to squelch. It spread as rapidly as the fire that would punish the convicted.

The condemned were sentenced to burn at the pyre within a matter of days. The mayor could see no other way to prevent a violent frenzy, even if he suspected that some of the accused were victims of false charges.

The more witches and wizards the townspeople saw burned, the more readily they attributed this particular type of evil to their neighbors. No one was truly safe from the reach of snowballing popular opinion, and social status frequently meant the difference between life and death.

Our family's title protected Gertrude and me, with our flaming red hair. Much of the region considered our hair color to be a mark of the Devil. Others saw it for the ludicrous assertion that it was. Either way, the memory of the last "witch" to be condemned was fresh in my mind.

She was a sweet girl, young like me. However, she was the daughter of the town baker. She lacked the protection my status afforded me. Her hair was straight where Gertrude's and mine curled, but it was just as red as ours.

The mayor drowned her, while her sanctimonious accusers cheered on what only they considered justice. The terms of her condemnation were illogical, yet common.

She was bound with chains and thrown into the lake. If she freed herself from her bindings and floated to the surface of the water, then she was clearly a witch, destined to burn at the pyre. If she couldn't break free of her chains, then she was a girl of pure soul.

The chains pulled the baker's daughter under the water. When she drowned, the mayor declared her a pure soul. She came up only when her broken father dove in to retrieve her body, the lake washing away the first of many tears he would shed.

As far as I knew, the only crime the baker's daughter had committed was to dare to be born with red hair and to be the unintended object of the blacksmith's affection. The accuser of the baker's daughter was also a girl, one who hoped to marry the blacksmith and saw the world as a harsh place, where she had to do what she must to forge ahead.

Father and Mother attempted to shield my sisters and me from the savage realities that took place in the town, just past the sloping hills of our estate, but the stories reached us anyway. Regardless, Father understood the dangers of tempestuous public opinion far better than we did.

He was cautious to the point of paranoia, all too aware of his life disappointments. He'd wanted only sons, yet all that remained to him were five daughters, and two of them had hair so bright it was impossible to conceal its abnormality.

He'd already lost his son and true heir long ago. He couldn't afford to lose me. Even if I was a distant second to my deceased brother, I was what he had to secure Norland Manor's future.

Under ordinary circumstances, Father wasn't a tolerant man. When witchcraft was involved, he was downright zealous. I found myself clenching in fear for Martha. Even if Father had visited Martha's kitchen as a boy as well, I knew his character. Allowances and exceptions were not Father's norm.

Maggie continued, and I felt my shoulders drop with her first words. "Lucky for Martha, his Lordship was desperate enough to take her seriously. He set about making very discrete inquiries into who this man was. When he found him, he ordered him to arrive after nightfall, cloaked, and not to tell anyone where he was going.

"When Marcelo asked his Lordship's permission to take you away so he could heal you in private, his Lordship was extremely agreeable. As you can imagine, he didn't want anyone to even suspect that he had willingly invited a magician into the Manor."

I nodded, absently. It wasn't just Martha that had taken a risk. Father had taken a big risk himself by involving a magician. I would have thought he and Mother would have preferred to let me die before attempting something like this.

"Marcelo?" I asked. "That's the magician's name?"

"As you know, Clara, I'd never disrespect a lord, and I think the magician is at least a lord—"

I raised my eyebrows at her in question.

"Well, I'm not sure that he is. There's something about him that makes me think he has good breeding. But no one ever introduced me or any of the other servants to him. Given the circumstances, I guess that's understandable. I don't know his family name or status, so I have no idea what to call him. I suppose I could ask him his name myself, but the chance hasn't come about, and he isn't the most approachable." Maggie was flustered.

"It's all right, Maggie. I understand." I was sure she didn't mean to be improper, not that I cared much about these kinds of formalities. "Continue with your story, please."

"Well, once Marcelo told his Lordship that chances were high that he could cure you, if only he could be left alone to his ways, your father gave his permission. No one else was giving you much of a chance at survival. The next day, they loaded you and me in the carriage. John drove the carriage instead of one of the usual horsemen. His Lordship didn't want anyone outside of the house to know.

"Marcelo met us at the lake house after we arrived. No one in Lake Creston knows we're here together except for Thomas, and Thomas doesn't know who Marcelo is. Besides, Thomas is a little slow."

Maggie saw the question in my face. "Thomas is the caretaker here."

Maggie sighed loudly. Mother would have been horrified at her manner and undoubtedly would have declared it unfit for a servant. "That's all that I know about Marcelo, Clara. And it's not very much at all."

I agreed. It wasn't, especially when it seemed like there was so very much to learn about him.

SWALLOWED WHOLE BY PERFECTLY
STILL WATER

*E*very muscle in my body ached. Even my bones hurt. Maggie didn't need to warn me to slow down. I had no real choice. My body couldn't support the activity my awakening brain longed for.

It was the first day without fever and already I was impatient, ready to move on. But there was little to do other than wait.

By the time dusk arrived, I could barely keep my eyes open. After a month of fitful sleep, I slept soundly. Not even the whisper of a dream interfered once I gave myself over to the dark of night.

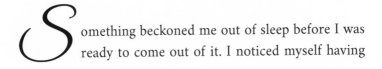

*S*omething beckoned me out of sleep before I was ready to come out of it. I noticed myself having thoughts again and realized I was awake. But why was I? I was still tired.

I flung back the covers, suddenly hot. I arranged the pillows behind me and sat, intending to steal a few moments of stillness before the activity of the day began.

But then I spotted Marcelo hidden within the shadows thrown by the fire.

He sat in the rocking chair Maggie had occupied the day before.

He was looking straight at me and appeared undisturbed by my startled reaction.

I stared back at him. I hadn't met anyone like him. Everything about him felt different. He appeared to lack a concern with etiquette that everyone else I knew possessed.

He didn't blink or look away. He didn't appear embarrassed that I'd caught him watching me while I slept.

In defeat, I closed my eyes to push him out. His gaze searched too intensely and left nowhere to hide.

When he stood, my eyes trailed him as he walked toward me. His cloak was absent. It was the first time I'd seen him without it. His body without the cloak didn't surprise me, its apparent agility matched the delineation of muscle visible through his shirt.

He reached my bedside and, in a replay of the day before, his eyes traveled the length of my body. His gaze left a flurry of sensations in its wake. My skin pricked and tingled again, abruptly reminding me that I was naked beneath my nearly translucent gown.

The thin cotton clung to my body and revealed everything. I pulled up the covers without knowing whether he realized why. His attention was absorbed, focused some-where else than on me as a person.

I wondered if and when he would speak.

Again, he looked to the corners of the chamber and then to the fire.

Again, he left without warning.

I waited, although this time I didn't count on his return.

~

Maggie came instead of Marcelo, and she helped me into a bath. I couldn't remember a time when the water felt that good as it embraced my body. The water eased my aching and quieted thoughts that kept trying to get ahead of themselves.

The hot water soothed my brain, frayed from a month of sporadic hallucinations. It also seemed to offer the promise of regaining my former self, though deep within I wasn't sure if I wanted to.

Before she left me alone, Maggie lit two candles to either side of the bath. The candlelight reflected on the water's surface, beginning to hypnotize me. I didn't resist. I followed the flames as they flickered and rippled.

I watched one flame until my eyes began to blur, and then I watched the other. Back and forth I went.

Then something unusual happened. The flames multi-plied across the water's surface.

First there were two flames. Then there were four. Then there were eight. Sixteen. Thirty-two. Then I lost count.

Flames burst all around me.

I barely breathed.

Soon, flames lit almost the entire surface of the water. It was breathtaking, like the sun glittering across the surface of the lake. But unlike the water of Lake Creston that rippled and moved, reflecting the life it contained, the water of the bath was as still as glass.

Mesmerized, I watched.

I didn't question whether this might be an alluring effect of a mind that had experienced too many feverish hallucinations.

There was no thought. Not a single one.

I observed, detached, void of emotion, until that final duplication.

Then I shouted out.

I writhed in pain, until the pain itself took mercy on me.

It overloaded my system, and I blacked out.

My last memory is of me slipping beneath the water's surface.

I fell and kept falling, heading toward the bottom of a body of water that had no visible end.

I slipped farther and farther away, swallowed whole by perfectly still water.

A FLOOD

I lost the rest of the day and awoke the next morning early with the sun. Before I even opened my eyes, I cringed at a searing pain that swept across my skin.

A moan brought Maggie and Marcelo running. As they appeared at my bedside, I realized I was in my bed again.

The look in Maggie's eyes told me something serious had happened. Concern danced clumsily across her features. She didn't know what to do to help me.

In contrast, Marcelo revealed almost nothing of his thoughts. But there was something different from the previous two times he'd stood looking at me; I just didn't know what it was.

"Ah." I winced in pain. My face contorted as I struggled to sit. Maggie reached out to help, but her attempts were ineffective.

She didn't know where to touch me. A thick film of ointment covered my entire body from the neck down, and thin bandages protected my skin wherever my nightgown did not.

In the end, I didn't sit. With or without Maggie's assistance, the pain was too great.

Finally, Marcelo spoke to me. "What happened?"

I looked at him, stunned. "You don't know what caused this?"

"No." For the first time, traces of concern flashed across his face. However, as quickly as they appeared, they vanished. Again, there was nothing.

My eyes grew hot, and I knew the tears were coming. "I need a moment to myself please," I said to them but looked toward the window. Even though it was closed to the dawning light outside, it was away from them and their piercing stares and probing questions.

Surprised, Marcelo turned and walked away. Maggie lingered, but met my wishes. She pulled the door closed behind her, but I still heard Marcelo's voice.

"We can give her some time, but not too long. I need to understand what happened to her as quickly as possible. Stay outside her door in case she needs you. I'll be back shortly to try again."

Maggie didn't say anything, but I heard her slide a chair across the floor.

I expected to hear the sound of a horse riding away, but there was none. Marcelo walked in a clipped pace to his chambers and closed the door.

Alone, I allowed myself to cry. The tears were hot with a frustration I didn't realize I'd been holding back until it burst forth like water crashing through an oppressive dam.

I cried because I didn't understand what was wrong with me, and now even the expert didn't know. I was tired of feeling achy and ill, of not being able to move around and do what I wanted.

I cried because I was alone, with no one to hold me. Gertrude was far away, and I wanted her to stay that way. I would never forgive myself if she fell ill because of me.

I cried because my parents wanted to marry me away to a bully and because they'd sent me off to the lake house with this man who made me uneasy. I cried because I didn't understand anything anymore and because I was very frightened. I cried, simply, because I hurt.

I let everything boil over until there was nothing left in me that needed to get out. I shut my eyes in exhaustion, and I willed the relief of sleep to claim me right then.

For once, it did as I asked.

KEEP THE SECRET

*T*he scene from the morning replayed itself. I woke again to find Maggie and Marcelo in my room. They rushed to me when they noticed me awake.

This time, the shutters were open and the midday sun filtered across the space, softening Marcelo's face, revealing a youthfulness I hadn't noticed before.

It seemed to soften his demeanor too. "How are you, Clara?" he asked.

I looked at him through swollen, vulnerable eyes and had nothing to say. My eyes threatened tears again and, though I resisted, they slipped through my grasp and rolled down my cheeks. They spoke for me.

"Oh, Clara, don't cry," Maggie said. "Marcelo will figure out what's wrong with you and get you fixed right up." Again, Maggie reached out to comfort me and reined her hands in. There was nowhere safe to touch. "Isn't that right, Marcelo?"

Because of the unusual circumstances and close quarters, Maggie treated Marcelo with uncommon informality. Marcelo ignored both her question and the breach in etiquette.

"Clara, how does your body feel?"

"My body?"

"Whatever happened to you in the bathtub burned you severely. All the skin that was submerged was burned. Your face and neck were unaffected. It would appear that the water burned you, yet I already checked the water, and it was unadulterated. Did something happen?"

"What do you mean the water burned me?"

"I don't know what else could have. You were naked in the water when it happened. You weren't touching anything, and there was nothing that could have done this near the bathtub. When I heard you scream, I rushed to the bath. I knocked, but you didn't answer. When I entered, you were unconscious and your face was underwater. I pulled you out of the tub and onto the floor and there you started breathing on your own. But you didn't regain consciousness again until this morning."

He paused for a moment, deliberating how to say what he wanted to say next, and in that moment, I synthesized all that he'd just said into "You were naked when I pulled you out of the tub." To think I'd been self-conscious when he saw me in my nightgown just yesterday.

I was trying to push away my discomfort at the thought of this inscrutable man both seeing and touching my naked body when he continued.

"I put my arms in the water to pull you out, and nothing happened to me. I felt only water, which was barely hot. It couldn't have burned you like this. At least, not without something else causing it. Are you sure nothing happened to explain this?"

I thought back. I remembered it all.

"Something did happen. But I don't think that it could have burned me. It's not possible."

"Go ahead, Clara. Tell me everything you remember, exactly as you remember. Don't leave out any details."

I nodded and drew breath before plowing ahead. It seemed like a bizarre thing to recount, like another of my feverish hallucinations.

"Well, I remember looking at the water and noticing the reflections of the flames of the candles Maggie had set by the tub. There were two of them. The more I stared at the reflections, the more the flames seemed to come alive. They danced and flickered. And then, they just started multiplying. I don't know why." I looked into Marcelo's eyes, searching for his reaction. This is where it began to get strange.

"Maggie, will you excuse us now?"

Maggie startled. I didn't expect Marcelo's request either. I could see that she wasn't happy about having to leave, but she did so anyway. As soon as she closed the door, Marcelo urged me to continue.

"The flames I saw in the water started becoming more and more until they almost covered the entire surface of the water."

Marcelo nodded, his attention rapt. Keep going.

"That's it. That's all I remember. The flames were about to cover the water completely when I blacked out. None of it makes sense. Was I imagining things again? Like when I had the fever?"

"Clara, tell me exactly how the flames reproduced themselves. Did they appear randomly across the surface of the water? Was there a pattern to it?"

I focused again until I could see it. "First there were two flames. Then there were four. Then eight and so on."

Marcelo seemed surprised by what I said, and his concentration increased.

"Does that mean something?"

"Hmm. It might. Did the reflection of the flames extend all the way down into the water?"

I shook my head. "No, at least not up until the point when I lost consciousness. The flames just covered the surface of the water. I remember thinking it looked like the sunset sparkling across Lake Creston, like it did when I got to watch it as a girl. There was barely any part of the water that wasn't covered with the reflection of the flames when I blacked out. But the flames were multiplying quickly. I assume that they completely covered the water by the time I passed out."

Marcelo didn't say anything. He was looking straight at me, but he wasn't focused on the *me* right there in front of him. He was studying the *me* of yesterday, determined to discover what could have caused water to burn me.

"What do you think?" I asked, attempting to bring him back. I needed to understand. The more I realized that even he didn't know what happened to me, the more frightened I became.

"I'm really not sure how this could've happened, Clara.

I'll have to think about it. I've never heard of something like this before. Especially not with someone like you."

I bristled, despite the seriousness of the situation. "Someone like me? What does that mean?"

"Nothing, nothing." He brushed it off, but it did mean something. "You'll need to stay here and rest as much as possible. The burns on your body are severe, and it'll take some time for them to heal. The more careful you are with yourself, the more likely it is that there'll be no serious scarring when this is all over."

"Scarring?" Oh no. "Will I be disfigured from this?"

"I don't think so. Not if you take it easy and allow your body to do what it knows best. But don't be fooled. The burns are serious. You need to rest for optimal recovery."

Great. More rest. As if I hadn't stayed in bed enough the last month. I sighed in frustration and tried to resign myself to Marcelo's recommendations.

"I'll monitor you closely, not only to make sure you heal properly, but to attempt to deduce what happened. In the meantime, you shouldn't worry too much. It's unlikely that anything like this will happen to you again. It was most likely an anomaly."

That wasn't very reassuring. He hadn't thought this could happen to me in the first place.

"And Clara, you can't tell anyone what happened in the water. No one. Not even Maggie."

He meant it. His tone was severe.

"Clara, you can't tell anyone at all. Are we clear on this?" His eyes bore into mine, trying to will my compliance with sheer force. The look on my face hadn't convinced him. No one had ever asked me to keep a secret like this one before.

"Why can't I tell Maggie?"

"I can't explain the reasons to you. You just need to know that you should not utter a word of this."

"You *can't* explain it to me, or you *won't* explain it to me?" I could appreciate that he was trying to help me, although my father undoubtedly was paying him generously for his efforts, but I didn't like him ordering me to keep secrets.

Maggie was my friend and helper. Surely, she would ask me what happened, and I didn't like having to lie to her. "If you want me to keep your secrets, you need to at least tell me why. You have to tell me something."

Irritation flashed across Marcelo's face before he stashed it away. "It's for your own good. You'll have to trust me on that. Or don't trust me and tell everyone you want. Then see what happens and how you like it."

I was at a disadvantage. I was the one who was sick and needed his help. I was the one who knew nothing at all about what was going on.

"What am I supposed to tell Maggie then? You know she'll ask me what happened."

"I needn't waste my time coming up with girlish stories. I have much more important things to tend to. Invent something."

Marcelo looked like he was about to leave.

"Wait. I want to ask something of you."

He stopped his retreat, huffed, and drew close to me again, impatient. His gaze was intent, and I almost lost my nerve. In that moment, he was the last person I wanted to have to ask a favor of, but what choice did I have? I swallowed and squeaked out the words.

"Please don't tell my parents that I'm better."

Dark eyebrows cocked in response.

"And why wouldn't I tell them you're recovering? They hired me to cure you, you know."

I steeled my nerve and rushed forward before I lost it. I didn't want to confide in him. He'd made it clear that he was neither my friend nor my ally and that he had no interest in becoming either of the two. But my parents would marry me off to Winston if he didn't help me. I looked away from him as I spoke, baring my heart out of necessity.

"Because if I recover during this next month, they're going to marry me away to an awful person. If they believe I'm still seriously ill by the end of this month, they'll have to withdraw from the arrangement. The other family has given them a deadline by which I must recuperate for the wedding to move forward. If I don't become well by that time, they'll marry their son to someone else."

There was a prolonged silence in which Marcelo said nothing.

"Please," I begged. "If my parents don't see me by that time and you don't tell them, I'll be spared a life of torment. Maggie won't tell them either."

Something swept across Marcelo's face that again I couldn't identify. But I saw something.

"Very well. I agree not to tell them that you're recovering. For now," he added, somewhat menacingly.

"Thank you." The thought that something good could come from all my suffering lifted my spirits immensely. In that moment, I didn't even care that Marcelo was unpleasant. An outcome that didn't see me married to Winston was enough to compensate for many inconveniences.

Marcelo tipped his head once and left the room. It was the closest thing to a farewell he'd given me yet.

He left the door open. I could hear him cross the house, leather-soled shoes slapping against stone tiles. Then, I heard a door close, shutting me and my questions out.

The sound was also a signal to Maggie. Within the minute, she rushed to my side. When I convinced her that I didn't know what had happened in the bathtub—and that was the truth—she was disappointed and went off to prepare some more broth for me.

These were going to be long days.

THE UNDENIABLE SOMETHING IS HAPPENING

J had no idea how intense the days were going to become. I couldn't possibly.

I didn't even make it through the week without more problems, serious problems. I was drowning under the weight of them.

I was still scheduled to marry into future unhappiness. Whether I married Winston or not largely depended on the good will of Marcelo, an insensitive magician I still knew next to nothing about. What I did know about him didn't do much to put my mind at ease. If anyone were to find out that I was at Lake Creston with a wizard, it would be bad, very bad.

Nothing good had ever come of magic that I was aware of, yet here I was, secluded with a man who apparently dedicated himself to magic. And now things that not even he could explain were beginning to happen to me.

And things were about to get worse.

My skin was healing nicely, and the pain wasn't as terrible as it had been at first, but my movement was still very limited. I hadn't been outside in so long that I couldn't remember when I'd last stood under the sun.

Marcelo was unwrapping my bandages, just as he did every day. It was an involved process. Maggie started by helping me up and over to the rocking chair. I sat gingerly on its edge until she stripped my bed of its sheets and fitted a clean one on the mattress. The soiled bedding sat in a pile waiting to be boiled. Marcelo didn't want to risk infection of my burns. Then Maggie helped me over to the bed again and pulled my nightgown off. She tossed it into the laundry pile.

She helped me onto the bed, onto my stomach, where I tried very hard to pretend that I wasn't laying naked in front of Marcelo. There was no alternative. He began the tedious process of unwrapping the bandages around my feet and legs. Then he unwrapped the bandages that protected my hands from infection.

"You've made great progress," he said, while he looked me up and down. "I think I can say surely now that there will be no scarring once this is over. The swelling has gone down, and there are no boils or blisters on your skin."

I picked up on subdued surprise in his voice. I turned my head to try to look over my shoulder at my back but couldn't really make out much. I'd noticed that my pain level had diminished.

Perhaps if I just ignored things, they'd go away. It wasn't a good plan, but it was a plan of sorts.

I was far out of my comfort zone.

I'd never been this gravely injured before. I couldn't guess how long my skin would take to heal.

Obviously, Marcelo did. "It's truly remarkable. Unheard of, in fact." He seemed to be talking more to himself now than to Maggie or to me. "I've never seen burns like yours not advance to the stage of painful blistering. Now that I think of it, your incredible progress is almost as unusual as the situation that caused the damage in the first place. Clara, have you done anything to speed the healing?"

"Me? No. What could I have done?"

"Turn around and lie on your back."

Maggie helped me flip over until I lay there as he asked, fully naked and exposed.

"It's amazing," he mumbled. "Does this still hurt?" I winced as he placed his hand flat against my thigh, expecting the searing pain I'd grown used to over the last few days. But I soon realized it didn't hurt as much as I thought it would. I relaxed.

"Yes, but not as much as it used to."

"How about here?" He touched the bottom and tops of my feet.

This time I didn't tense in anticipation. "The same. It still hurts, but not as much."

"And your private areas? Are they very sore still?"

I cringed inwardly at the fact that this man was even mentioning my private areas, but he had good reason to. The fire had burnt the parts of my body with particularly sensitive skin the most. The pain was dreadful.

"Yes, they're still quite sore. But they too are better." This was news I was very happy to report, even if I didn't understand it. All of my body was healing rapidly, even those parts that had been most damaged.

"Maggie, begin spreading the ointment."

"Yes, Sir." Maggie moved to retrieve the ointment Marcelo had kept warming by the fireside.

Marcelo had the modesty to allow a woman to touch my body instead of him, but he hovered over Maggie to ensure she did the job properly. "Make sure the layer of ointment is as thick as before. We need her to continue healing at this speed if she can."

But the ointment had little to do with my rate of healing. I think Marcelo suspected this even then.

"Can I sit in front of the fire for a while? It's incredibly boring to be in this bed all day long."

"I think that would be all right. But only for a little while. If you tire, let us know right away. Besides, I don't think your bottom will like sitting in a hard, wooden chair for very long."

He was right. I hadn't thought of that. My bottom stung, bright red as it was.

Even so, bandaged and dressed in a fresh nightgown, Maggie helped me to the rocking chair. She had piled blankets on the seat as a cushion, and I sunk in. It felt good to have a change of scenery, even if my vantage point had only changed by a few feet.

"Thank you, Maggie." I smiled encouragingly at her. These had been difficult weeks for me, but I knew they'd been for her as well. She was the one responsible for meeting my every need and keeping me safe. She was my friend and she had to watch me suffer. She was away from the home she'd known her entire life, away from her mother, with no one to talk to while I was unwell. None of it could have been easy for her.

I caught her eye. "For everything."

She smiled. "You're welcome, Clara. Shall I leave you alone for a bit to enjoy the fire in quiet?"

"Yes, please. That sounds wonderful."

The fire rewarded my appreciation with a spectacular show of sparks as a log fell to one side. It settled down again, and the flames danced and mesmerized me as they always did. Just as water was hypnotic to me, so was fire. I could stare at it for hours—if my injured backside allowed.

I eased back into the chair and let my gaze blur. In seconds, my mind was ablaze with vibrant oranges, yellows, and even indigos. It was breathtakingly beautiful. I no longer distinguished the fire I was looking at from the fire within. It all made me feel content.

I leaned my head against the wooden back of the chair and closed my eyes. I was pleased to discover that the fire remained. It danced as brilliantly as before.

Somewhere, a part of my brain registered Maggie running toward Marcelo's rooms, but I continued to enjoy the display uninterrupted.

When Marcelo rushed into my bedroom and closed the door behind him so that Maggie wouldn't follow, I was at peace.

It was Marcelo's frantic voice that shattered it. "Clara! Stop this!"

I opened my eyes. Despite his frenetic order, I was calm.

Then I saw that fire had sprung up all around me. It licked at the massive stone hearth, burning the wooden ledge that crowned it. Flames snaked across the stone floor, reaching for me with their wily, tantalizing ways.

I screamed. The fire would be at my feet in seconds. My skin stung, reminding me of the damage already done, warning me of the fire's power. I screamed again.

"Clara, look at me. Right now." Marcelo's tone left no room for argument or disobedience. I looked at him.

"You're doing this. And you need to stop it right now."

As strange as his statement was, I found myself nodding and shifting back toward the approaching fire. I looked at it and tried to get it to stop. But I couldn't. I was panicking. I wasn't connected to it in the same way anymore.

"Do something. It's about to reach me!" I was freaking out.

"Clara, make it stop." But Marcelo had barely gotten the words out when he realized I wasn't going to be able to stop it.

It would reach me in seconds.

Marcelo sped to my side, extended his hands, palms toward the approaching fire, and spoke.

"We honor you for your might, Fire. We thank you for your existence and for all that you do."

The heat of the fire seeped through the bandages on my toes, while the fire continued its probing crawl toward me.

"But you cannot harm this girl. There is no call for destruction here. There is no call for harm. Put that side of you to rest. Stop. Now."

And to my astonishment, the fire did.

It retreated as evenly as it had come. It crawled back, slithering across the hot tile floor and down the stone walls surrounding the hearth, until, progressively, it was nothing more than the flames one would expect to find in a lake house fireplace.

If not for the blackened wooden ledge above the hearth, smoldering, and a thin film of black soot that coated the stone of the hearth and the floor, I would have convinced myself that I'd imagined everything. Its implications were alarming.

I stared ahead at the modest fire, stunned and speechless. Then I brought my hands to my face and burst out in tears. My body shook uncontrollably.

I'd been a strong, relatively independent, private young woman. But since Marcelo came into my life, I'd swooned, screamed, and wept like a fragile girl incapable of caring for herself.

None of that mattered to me now though. I was more frightened than I'd ever been in my life.

It wasn't just that the fire had almost burned me again, and it wasn't that the firewater or whatever-it-was had burned me already. I wasn't scared because of the fever that took me out of my mind for so long or because I was far away from home.

I was almost paralyzed with fear because I didn't understand what was happening to me, and now I couldn't deny that something was.

And the only person capable of helping me understand

any of it scared me almost more than all of the rest put together.

Yet, I crumpled into his arms when he wrapped them around me.

WHO OR WHAT AM I?

"*D*o you feel well enough to move back to the bed?"

My sobs had subsided and the inset of exhaustion weighed my arms down heavily around Marcelo's waist. I nodded.

He helped me stand, and I limped awkwardly over to the bed. I rolled onto it and lay there, slack. Not a single question hampered my mind. I was too tired and too weak.

Outside, Maggie couldn't take it any longer. Her place as a servant obligated her to be silent and stay out of the way unless she was called upon or expected. But she'd been the first one to see the fire spreading. And since Marcelo had closed the door in her face, she didn't know what had happened. She'd heard me crying again.

"Sir!" she yelled through the door. "Is everything all right?"

"Yes, Maggie. You may come in."

Maggie had the door open before he finished his

sentence. She rushed to my side. For her, I opened my eyes. "I'm fine, Maggie. I'm fine." I tried to smile.

Maggie threw herself on me, forgetting my burns. She hugged me before my groans reminded her of the situation.

"Thank you, Maggie. I appreciate you."

What I censored was the last part of this statement, what I was truly thinking. *I appreciate you even though I have no idea who or what I am anymore.*

ANOTHER WAY OF LIFE

*T*he days came and went, looking much the same. I lay in bed, where my only job was to heal, while Marcelo whipped around me like a whirlwind.

After the last incident, he didn't leave the lake house again, anxious I might start another fire. Since I didn't know how I'd done it either time, we couldn't anticipate if or when it would happen again.

While I rested, Marcelo studied. He studied books and he studied me, and he stared off into the distance analyzing it all. Gradually, books piled up on one of the side tables. From the bed, I couldn't see their titles, and I regretted it. Had I been well, I would have tried to peek inside the books. Their exteriors were dark and mysterious much like their owner. Marcelo had given me few answers, and I suspected that his books would tell me more than he was willing to share.

Whenever Marcelo wasn't there with me, Maggie was.

She slept on a cot, between the fire and me. I assumed this was Marcelo's attempt at insulating me from the flames.

I hoped it would work.

On my end, while I allowed my body to heal itself, I focused on not thinking about the fire in the fireplace, or the fire in the water, or the fire anywhere else. But I quickly discovered the problem with not thinking about something: It seemed to make you think of it all the more.

It was late morning and already I'd grown bored of watching Marcelo pace back and forth across the room. He walked tirelessly, occasionally muttering to himself and sometimes stopping to reference a book. I knew he was trying to solve the question that I'd become, and I didn't figure it was a good sign that it was taking him this long to discover the answer.

"Marcelo?"

He continued as if he hadn't even heard me.

"Marcelo."

He looked up, confused, as if he'd forgotten where he was. Then his eyes focused, and he stopped walking to face me, his shirt open around the collar. Everything about him was either distracted or tousled.

"Will you please talk to me?"

He scratched the dark stubble that marked a two-day old beard and resigned himself. "Yes, I suppose I should talk it over with you. I can't make any sense of it otherwise. This just isn't the way things are supposed to happen."

He pulled up the rocking chair and sat on the edge of the seat, started to speak, then stopped. He rose to shut the door.

"Clara, I'm afraid that once I tell you what I've been considering all these days, you'll never be able to go back to your life the way it was before."

"I—"

"I know you think your life is already different and that you can't return to the way it was anyway." I tried to interrupt again but he held up his hand. "But it's not really that different. I could teach you to prevent what happened here with the fire so that it never happens again. You could return to Norland and lead a perfectly normal, healthy life. I think that whatever we do here should consider that to be your goal. Which means I'll have to be very careful of what I tell you."

Before he even finished, I was shaking my head. "What kind of a life do you really think awaits me at Norland? The way you speak, dress, and carry yourself—you must come from a wealthy family too. You know what it's like. What kind of a life do you think I lead, always being told what to do and when to do it? Continuously being told that I'm not and can never be as good as my dead brother because I'm a girl?

"If I'm not made to marry Winston, I'll be forced to marry somebody else. I'll go from being the obedient property of my parents to being the obedient property of my husband. Is it that surprising that I want more for my life?"

"No. I suppose not. But is this what you want for your life?"

I didn't know exactly what *this* was, but I had some ideas. I'd done everything possible to resist thinking of magic as the source of what had happened to me.

A life that magic touched in any way was undoubtedly a terribly dangerous one. As much as I didn't appreciate how Father and Mother had raised me, I understood why they shielded my sisters and me from magic. Retribution for involvement in magic arrived swiftly, unannounced, and with a vengeance that brooked no forgiveness.

Yet, I had nothing to do while in bed this last week but lose myself between alternating thoughts and stillness. While Marcelo paced furiously, I eventually surrendered to the ideas that insisted on coming.

I turned the little I knew about him and what happened to me over in my mind. I had many theories, and every single one intersected with the dangerous M word sooner or later.

None of them led to a normal life. All of them would horrify Father and Mother.

Nevertheless, they were vastly preferable to the vapid life I'd just described to Marcelo.

"I prefer it to the life lined up for me at Norland." I met his gaze. "Wouldn't you?"

Emotion flared in his expression before it passed. I hoped someday I would learn what went on behind that façade. "Yes, I would."

He slid back in the chair and crossed his arms across his chest. "You're certain?" His eyebrows crunched a fraction of an inch higher on his forehead. He didn't take any of this lightly. In fact, I hadn't seen him take anything lightly yet.

I nodded in affirmation while my heart pitter-pattered furiously. I didn't know what I was getting myself into. I was scared again. But, in truth, I wasn't as frightened as I would have thought.

The prospect of a different life excited me. There was little I would regret leaving behind.

Another way of life was choosing me.

LIFE AND DEATH SERIOUS

*M*arcelo sent Maggie away under the pretext that the errand was too important to entrust to Thomas. He told me she wouldn't be back until almost dark and that was barely enough time to get started. I tingled in anticipation of discovering what my new life held.

My burns were healing well, and I was able to sit up straight in bed without his assistance. "I'm ready."

"All right," he said, though he didn't sound convinced. Regardless, he began, and once he did, I was riveted.

"Clara, this isn't usually the kind of conversation one has. There's no easy or right way to say any of this." He ran his hands through messy hair. "I think what happened with you and the fire these two times was that you were doing magic."

He let his statement sink in. He understood better than I the prejudice, varying in degrees from dislike to murderous hostility, that magic brought along with it.

I answered softly and steadily; there was no point to denying the unavoidable conclusion. "How could *I* have done magic, without having any idea how?"

"That's the exact question I've been asking myself. It makes no sense. This isn't the way magic is learned. Regardless, that's the inescapable conclusion at which I've arrived. You did magic."

"Is magic what you did to make the fire retreat?"

He nodded. "Yes. It is."

"You really are a magician then?"

It was a superfluous question, one that looked for any way to deny what was rapidly becoming fully undeniable.

Marcelo didn't respond, although the look on his face said it all.

"So you're a wizard." My voice had taken on a tone of matter-of-fact resignation that went contrary to the titillating excitement of the forbidden and mysterious that naturally imbued magic. It was all happening fast. And I was utterly and completely unprepared for the turn my life was taking.

"If I'm a wizard, then I'm a very young and inexperienced one."

He didn't look *that* young. He only appeared to be a few years older than me. And I much doubted he was *that* inexperienced.

"I don't call myself a wizard or a magician or a sorcerer. In the end, they all do magic. Perhaps in different ways, but with similar tools. And what importance does a title have anyway?"

Among the nobility, titles meant everything. It was a fresh and novel concept to deny them importance.

Numbly, I spoke. "Are you implying that I'm a witch?" I enunciated each of the words thinking that if the towns-people even suspected someone of being a witch, they would call for execution amongst mounting hysteria.

His expression turned sad. "You don't want to be one, do you?"

His response wasn't exactly a denial, but it wasn't a confir-mation either. I took hold of this small hope, an infinitesimal gap within his answer, and attributed to it the possibilities of a chasm. Even if I could do a bit of accidental magic, perhaps I wasn't a *witch*. The word was so frightening that I couldn't bring myself to say it again. I had only once heard it tumble from Father's lips, but then it was with repulsion. I didn't want to give Marcelo the chance to attach this label to me.

I didn't really know if I wanted to be a witch or not. I could only assume that I didn't. The implications of such a thing were horrendous.

There was one thing that I was certain of, however. If there was even the smallest of chances that I was a witch, no one should ever find out.

"Marcelo, I honestly don't understand all of this. It's so… strange. And unexpected. Do you have a theory as to how I could have done magic without knowing how?"

"I have several. But the one I think most probable is that the fever somehow activated you. It's unheard of for someone to have a fever as intense as the one you had for long. In a few days, in a few hours even, either the person recovers or dies. But you, you endured the fever for nearly a month. The fever burned extremely hot. Yet you survived it.

"I don't know if there are many, or any, people alive right now that have lived through what you did. So I don't know if this is a common result of a prolonged fever or if it just happened in your case. It would make sense."

Make sense? None of this made any sense to me.

"I believe the fever created pathways to that part of your brain that can do magic intuitively, without training, because magic is a natural way of interacting with the elements and with all life. Nothing more.

"I can teach you how to control fire just enough so that it doesn't burn you again. Or you can try to forget everything I've told you. There's a chance that the pathways the fever opened in you will close again with time. In that case, you won't need to worry about the fire at all."

"I thought we already covered this. I want you to teach me," I blurted without thinking. Once I heard the words outside of me, I was certain of my choice.

Marcelo nodded. "I realize we already covered this. I wanted to give you another chance to change your mind. There's no going back once you walk this path. And I can't make any promises as to where this path will take you."

He looked me in the eyes. Blue bore into amber, trying to impose the severity of this fork in the road upon me.

"This is serious, Clara. Life and death serious."

I gulped. I nodded. I knew how serious it was. You couldn't live in Norland and not be aware of the dangers that accompanied association with magic, even if your parents tried to isolate you from all information about it.

Marcelo sighed heavily; I could hear the conflict that raged within him. But ultimately, his eyes spoke of resignation.

"If you want my honest opinion—"

I nodded encouragingly.

"Well, I think that you might not have any other real choice but to learn enough magic to protect yourself. Fire is powerful. It can be extremely dangerous. It's possible that only learning some basic magic will keep you safe from more experiences like those you've already suffered."

"And then, after, will you teach me more? Will you teach me all about magic?"

He was shaking his head even before I asked my second question.

"No, absolutely not, Clara. Magic isn't something to play with. I'll teach you only so that you can be safe and fully recover, because that's my responsibility right now. But I won't teach you more.

I didn't respond. His talk had regained its biting edge. I'd returned to being one more thing he needed to deal with.

With difficulty, I tried to rein my emotions in to see if I could draw more information out of him before he decided that even this conversation was a waste of his valuable time.

"Have you understood how it is that I could have made water burn me? How I could have made water turn into fire?"

"No," he admitted, his shoulders rounded in defeat. "I can only do that kind of magic intentionally. No one I'm aware of has ever been able to achieve the transformation of elements, make one element behave like another or join with another so harmoniously, without purposefully trying to do so.

"And there's also the point that the fire-water didn't act like fire with me. When I reached in the bath to retrieve you, my skin felt only water. Why did the water act like fire only with you? And why would this magic of extraordinary level appear within you, someone who has no inclination toward it?"

I got a glimpse of what had been swirling through his head while he paced my chambers. It was no wonder that he felt maddened by his fruitless exploration.

Even as my mind absorbed the many unanswered questions, a fleeting thought—a memory, actually—teased me, just out of reach. I struggled to grasp it, but it was not yet time. It would come, I hoped. Because even though I didn't know what it was, it was important.

A FIRST BOOK OF MAGIC

The day couldn't get any prettier. Finally, after having been in bed for so long, I was outside. Marcelo said I was well enough to have short visits outdoors, as long as Maggie stayed with me at all times.

The dressings had come off, and my feet were bandaged only when I needed to walk. The rest of the time, my skin was allowed to heal, exposed to the air.

I didn't realize how much the bandages had constrained me until Marcelo removed them. I felt gloriously free in no more than my thin, loose nightgown.

I didn't bother with modesty around Marcelo anymore. He'd already seen more than he could possibly forget, so I concerned myself only with my own comfort.

The sunshine was as splendid as if I were discovering its warmth for the first time. I rested on a clean blanket and longed for the day that my skin healed enough that Marcelo would allow it to come in contact with grass.

"How I love being outside, Maggie," I told her for the umpteenth time.

She chuckled. "It is quite lovely." She hadn't grown tired of my repeated comments yet.

"Clara, cover yourself."

"What is it?" I said while I folded the blanket over me. I followed Maggie's gaze to a man walking toward us. He was still too far away for me to make out who it was.

"It's Thomas. He must be returning from town."

We watched his calm gait in silence until he finally reached us.

"Hullo Maggie. Hullo Miss."

"Hello Thomas," Maggie said. "This is Lady Clara."

"Oh excuse me, Milady. I didn't know. Uh, I came over here because there was a delivery, Miss Maggie. The delivery man ran into me and gave it to me to give to you."

"Thank you, Thomas. May I have it please?"

"Yes, of course." He fumbled in his satchel until he emerged with a letter. Even from where I was I could make out the Count of Norland's seal.

"Is that all, Thomas?"

He nodded. "Yea it is. Good day then, Milady, Miss Maggie."

"Good day to you, Thomas," we said.

With thoughts of dread as to what official correspondence might mean, we watched him walk toward the stables. There were two weeks left for my parents to meet the Count of Chester's deadline. There was still a chance they could marry me to Winston.

"Can we burn it without reading it?"

Maggie chuckled. "You know we can't."

I groaned.

The sunshine didn't seem as magnificent anymore.

~

*M*aggie and I deliberated for only a minute as to whether or not I should open the letter before handing it over to Marcelo.

"Maggie," I'd told her, "I need to open this letter."

"Clara, you can't. You know how much trouble you'll get into for interfering with his Lordship's correspondence."

"Yes, but that's only *if* Father finds out. He won't find out."

"How can you be sure? Marcelo might tell him."

"He might. But I have a feeling he won't."

"And if he does?"

I shrugged. "Then he does. But I need to read the letter regardless."

Maggie's eyes were narrowed.

"Father is deciding my life, and I'm not even allowed to read about it? It's not right, Maggie."

"I don't know, Clara."

"You don't need to worry. I take full responsibility for opening the letter. Oops," I said while I slid my finger under the blood red seal of the House of Norland.

It cracked. The action was irreversible. "Now it's done, Maggie. So there's no point in worrying about it any longer."

She sighed loudly, but ultimately drew nearer to study the letter over my shoulder.

Predictably, the letter inquired about my health and asked Marcelo whether I would recover in time to meet the cutoff date for the wedding. I didn't know what Marcelo had told Father up until then, but whatever it was, it was clear that Father was unaware of how well I was doing, and for that I silently thanked Marcelo. I hoped he was willing to continue the charade a bit longer.

Maggie and I stayed outside as long as we could, but even the bright sunshine wasn't enough to ward off the chill of the winter afternoon. Spring was near, but not quite here. We had to go inside.

My chambers were warm and inviting, with bright sunlight filtering in through the windows and a small fire burning in the hearth. Maggie settled me into the rocking chair.

"You rest up while I go deliver this letter to Marcelo."

I flung myself upright in the rocking chair, awkwardly trying to stand while being careful of my injured feet. "No, Maggie. I'll go."

"Clara, don't be silly. You can barely stand."

I couldn't argue with that plain observation. "But Maggie, I have to be the one to take it to him. What if he takes issue with the letter's previous, uh, readership? I don't want him to get cross with you."

"I won't let him."

I looked at Maggie. She was spirited and brave and obviously, in this case, a bit of a fibber. She couldn't prevent Marcelo's anger any more than I could.

"Promise me that if he gives you any problems, you'll tell him to come speak with me at once."

"I promise, Milady," Maggie said, and she was off before I could protest any further.

I expected Maggie to rejoin me once she completed the task, but Marcelo came to see me instead. He didn't mention the letter at all but set about ensuring that my skin was still healing at its remarkable pace. I didn't say anything about Father's letter either. I had no choice but to trust Marcelo and hope for the best. I'd already argued my case with him. I would gain no advantage by doing it another time.

"How are you feeling today, Clara?"

"Better. It was wonderful to go outside again after so long."

I thought he might smile—his mouth twitched—but then he didn't. "And your feet? Does the skin still hurt when you put your weight on them?"

"My feet still hurt, though it's not as bad as it was before. It helps when I can lean some of my weight on Maggie while I walk." I regretted having to make this admission. My mind had moved past my body's current limitations.

"I have some books separated for you that I'd like you to study. You can read, right?"

I blinked at him, letting the moment pass, trying hard not to say something snarky. I blinked another time. "Of course I can read. What kind of books are they?"

"The dangerous kind," he grumbled.

At Norland Manor, Father had a sophisticated-looking library, but he and his predecessors had collected its contents mostly for show. I devoured many of the books that lined the floor-to-ceiling shelves, but none of them was as interesting as Marcelo's promised to be.

I relished the thought of perusing books of magic. I never imagined I would, and the unexpected surprise was delightful. My innocence impeded a complete under-standing of the gravity of the situation Marcelo and I were entering together.

"Are you ready to study now?"

I nodded, bright and eager. I couldn't hear what he muttered under his breath as he turned and walked away.

He returned quickly, carrying only one book. "You must promise to take good care of it. This book is very old. It won't withstand misuse."

He held it against his chest, unwilling to part with it until I promised.

"Marcelo, I promise that I'll be very careful with the book. I've read old books in my father's library. I know how to handle them."

"This book isn't like most other old books. It's special to me for many reasons. I wish I didn't have to let you look at it, but I'm convinced it's the best one for you to start with."

He still hadn't handed over the book.

I looked him straight in the eyes and said, "No harm will come to the book while in my care."

I hoped I was right. I couldn't be sure the book wouldn't spontaneously combust in my grip after my experiences with fire since my arrival at the lake house.

He handed over the book with a reluctant sigh. It was big and heavy, and I immediately liked how it felt in my hands. It had a particular smell to it: a combination of old paper and dust, which I expected, but there was also something else. I couldn't tell what it was, but it smelled spicy, almost like cloves, like when Martha made spice bread for the holidays and the scent of cloves, nutmeg, and ginger filled the kitchen for days.

"*The Magyke of the Elementes*." The title scrolled across the cover in gilded, ornate lettering. Swirls consumed the front of the book. "This looks amazing, Marcelo. Thank you."

His anxiety didn't abate with my appreciation. "You can't let Maggie get too close to the book. She can't touch it or look at it."

"All right." I had no idea what I would say to her when she asked about the book, because she would ask, but I knew better than to look to Marcelo for suggestions.

"I'll retrieve the book from you every evening before you sleep, and I'll keep it in my rooms so that it's safe. When your study of this book is complete, I'll bring you another one."

"Is there anything in particular I should focus on?"

"Yes. You need only read the sections about the element of fire, since that's where our concern with you lies. You can skip the rest."

I nodded and balanced the book on my lap. I didn't even notice Marcelo leave as I opened my first book of magic.

YOU ARE WHO YOU BECOME

I read for the rest of the afternoon and then by candlelight into the evening. Maggie checked on me often, always trying to peek at the contents of the book while doing so, but I managed to keep the secret.

When Maggie asked what I was reading, I still hadn't thought of what to tell her, so I opted for the truth—sort of. I told her it was Marcelo's book, which he'd given me to read so I wouldn't be bored anymore, and that he'd told me that no one else could look at it or touch it.

When Maggie raised her eyebrows at that, I just shrugged in a you-know-how-strange-Marcelo-can-be kind of fashion. She didn't much like that, but she accepted it. She took care of the tasks that had been piling up while she tended to me, and I read happily, grateful finally to have a serious distraction from my body's recovery.

The book had to be centuries old, and I poured over its every detail. I ignored Marcelo's instruction to limit myself to the chapters that discussed fire. I couldn't help myself.

My brain raced ahead of me, attempting to take it all in at once, thirsting for any new knowledge. It wouldn't let me skip a word.

Everything about the book ignited my curiosity, particularly the dedication scrawled in a messy hand at the front. It said:

To my dear Marcelo,
May this book guide you better than it did me.

Remember, if you have it within you, you do not need it outside of you.

This book will guide you toward what you already know.
Yours always,
Albacus

Who was Albacus? And how long ago had he written this inscription, its ink feathering with age, each letter appearing to have its own aura of faded sepia ink.

I was a fast reader and had moved far beyond the inscription by the time Marcelo came to collect his book for the night.

"What do you think?" he asked.

"I love it."

His outward expression said he doubted this, but his eyes told me he was secretly pleased. Marcelo was a man of a great many contradictions, especially since I didn't know him well enough to discern the deeper meaning of his words and actions.

"Did you read much?"

I hedged my answer carefully. I didn't want him to know that I was reading the whole book until I'd already done so. At this point, he didn't know how rapidly I could read.

"I read the entire time since you gave me the book, and I'm learning a lot. But that's fairly easy, since I knew absolutely nothing about magic before you lent me the book."

"Do you have any questions that came up from your reading?"

"Oh, I have lots, but none that need answering now. Perhaps if I keep reading, the book itself might answer some of them. Whatever questions survive once I've finished, I can ask you then. If that's all right with you," I added, reminding myself who was the teacher here and who was the pupil.

He studied me. He didn't hide what he was doing. He looked me up and down while he deliberated. "Yes, that will be fine. We'll speak of it at the end." His tone of voice was hesitant, as if he were suspicious of something more significant than my reading sections he'd suggested I skip.

"How are your burns feeling tonight? Has there been any change?"

"No change. They're about the same."

"Well, get some good rest. You need it."

"Good night, Marcelo," I said to his back as he walked out the door.

The beautifully illustrated illuminations from the book —most of them alchemical representations— flashed through my mind, and I sensed they would follow me into my sleep. Perhaps there my inexperienced mind could make more sense of them.

~

*P*lants walked my dreams, and unusual-looking humans walked alongside them, some of them with body parts of an animal nature.

Humans and near-humans danced beneath bright moonlight, laughing raucously. A fire burned within the circle they created through linked appendages.

I realized they were laughing at the fire, and with that realization the fire acted.

The fire spread furiously and quickly. It burned across the expanse between the bonfire and the circle of dancers in a heartbeat. The flames licked at the creatures, determined to show them who was most powerful.

There were no screams. The creatures continued to laugh while they burned and disfigured.

The fire spared only one.

The creature—no, a man—moved closer until he fully obscured everything taking place behind, blotting out the twisting and melting figures. He wore a mask that covered the top half of his face. A large beak of a nose, painted a bright violet, distracted from the features I could recognize. Black plumes flared at the hairline, ostentatious as they swayed.

But then I took in eyes and lips. Blue eyes, so bright they appeared to be glowing. A wide mouth with full lips.

It was Marcelo.

The instant I realized it, the dream came crashing to a close, a portal sucking shut, a vacuum collapsing on itself. And out of the nothingness that my dream was rapidly becoming, I heard Marcelo's echoing words.

I am coming for you. You are who you become.

THE ELEMENTS WITHIN US

I woke, startled and flushed. Faint light outlined the shutters, telling me the sun had only just risen. I pushed onto my elbows and looked around the room that had become so familiar to me in the last weeks.

Maggie slept on a cot, positioned strategically before the fire. The fire's tendrils illuminated her face in constantly shifting patterns.

I began to settle. My heart beat more slowly. The dream had disturbed me, and I didn't even understand what it had all meant. It had been unusually bizarre.

I didn't want to wake Maggie, so I sat as still as I could and reviewed what I'd studied in *The Magyke of the Elementes* the day before. What impacted me the most was the author's insistence that all of the elements were already present within us, so it was natural to work with them.

The book argued that water made up most of our bodies. This was news to me, and I marveled at how something as solid as our bodies consisted of something as fluid as water. Because water was such a significant part of us, it was the easiest to learn to manipulate, and the novice pupil should begin there.

Obviously, I hadn't. I'd inadvertently interacted with fire before understanding anything that *The Magyke of the Elementes* insisted was imperative to know before delving into this most dangerous yet rewarding art of magic.

The book warned that if the student didn't comprehend the nuances of fire and treat it with the honor it deserved, the consequences would be disastrous.

But fire, like water, was also within us, though not in as great a measure. Fire was innately more volatile than water, so we had less of it. Fire was evident in our passions and anger, and it was within the spark that was responsible for the beating heart of life.

Earth and air were also a part of us. Our bodies were of the earth, our spirits of the heavens. Our mothers birthed us into a lifetime on earth, to walk it and hopefully to leave it better than we found it. When we died, our bodies returned to the earth. From beginning to end, it was indelibly tied to our existence.

And just as the element of earth defined our lives, so did the element of air, as human beings had both a body and a spirit. One couldn't exist without the other; a person had to possess both to live.

Air was as integral to our beings as any of the other elements, though it was the easiest to overlook, invisible to the eye.

Any single one of these four basic elements was incredibly powerful and could be devastatingly destructive. Water could form tsunamis, floods, and ice storms, extinguishing life quickly, or it could withhold its nurturing and most life would fall victim to drought.

Many cultures contained legends of ancient floods that wiped out most of humanity, as it was with the story of Noah and his Ark. The ways in which water would transform and cause harm if it so chose were too many to mention.

Fire could burn its way through almost anything, killing as it spread. It might come from the sky, the spark of lightning setting ablaze the ground. It could rumble and sputter within the earth, threatening explosions of molten lava. It might devastate entire regions, bringing all life to a halt.

Earth could shake and split, opening up vast, gaping wounds in its crust and swallowing any life. Earth could shake us like a dog shakes its fleas. It could deny its fertility so that food wouldn't grow.

Like the other elements, air could be equally annihilating. Hurricanes and tornadoes ravaged anything in their path, and even the slightest imbalance of air would devastate a human being who relied on the breath to survive.

Each of the fundamental four elements contained the opposing potentials for nourishment and devastation.

Within a student who took care to balance body, mind, and spirit, the four elements coexisted harmoniously. But in the absence of equilibrium, any of the elements might flare, causing the person to display unhealthy destructive emotions and actions.

The Magyke of the Elementes insisted that it was only a pupil who possessed emotional, mental, physical, and spiritual health that should consider engaging in elemental magic. The book warned that danger likely awaited the student who moved forward without ensuring this prerequisite.

However, these dire warnings did nothing to scare me away from learning more. On the contrary, I was so anxious to continue reading that I found myself hoping Maggie would rise soon so that Marcelo would bring me the book again.

Before long, Maggie granted my unspoken wish. She began to stir, and the day suddenly looked much brighter.

I cautiously observed the fire while I waited for her to waken fully. I wanted to reach out to the fire, to engage it, to see what secrets it would share with me.

The flames eagerly responded, rising a bit higher. A wave of fear rushed through me and temporarily quelled my enthusiasm.

There was no way around it. I would have to wait to learn more.

THE UNIQUE PATH

*T*he day came and went much like the one before and much like the next. I was so engrossed in my reading that I forgot about the pain and the discomforts of bed rest. By the third day of reading, *The Magyke of the Elementes* suggested exercises for the initiate to begin engaging the elements. After my experience with fire, I knew it wise to wait for Marcelo to try any of the practice lessons.

Nevertheless, despite the nagging guilt that told me I was doing something I shouldn't, I tried the briefest and easiest practice lesson. I couldn't help myself.

I was alone in my room. Marcelo had checked on me that morning, and he likely wouldn't again until after lunch. Maggie had just left, telling me she was off to do the laundry. Chances were as good as they got that I would be undisturbed.

A pitcher of water was on the bedside table. I snuck one last glance at the door before I focused my gaze on the water inside it. As encouragement for the exercise, the book reminded the reader that the secret to doing magic was in understanding that the elements were already within us. We controlled them every day—unconsciously—but, by focusing will and mind, we could bridge the few steps between the unconscious and conscious levels.

I stared at the water like I had the fire, until my gaze blurred and I no longer noticed its details, until I no longer thought much about what I was doing at all. And as I looked at it, the water sloshed once and then diminished to waves and later ripples.

I observed the water as it took its time returning to stillness. The waves and ripples lessened so gradually, so minutely, that I thought they had no end.

Finally, however, all indication of motion ceased.

The water's movement had been minor, but there could be no doubt that I'd caused it. There was no other explanation for it. The pitcher sat, just as it had, physically undisturbed by its environment.

I didn't try to suppress the grin that spread across my face. I experienced the greatest joy I'd felt in a long time. My entire body tingled with excitement, at a vague sense of accomplishment and at the potential of what was to come.

I was capable of doing magic.

How had I not known this until Marcelo came into my life?

$\sim$

*W*hen Marcelo came to retrieve the book that night, I worked hard to contain my excitement. I still had another day of reading left, and I didn't want to do anything that might interfere with my ability to continue.

I suspected Marcelo might be displeased with me when he learned that I hadn't limited my reading to the chapters about fire. But it was worth the risk; I felt that more strongly now than I had before. What the book was teaching me was invaluable, if only because one of its exercises had already shown me that my abilities extended beyond fire into water.

"How's the reading going?" He no longer began his queries with my physical health. I imagined he was as curious as I was about what it would be like for him to instruct me in magic, even if he only wanted to teach me the minimal.

"It's going great." I smiled and tried to conceal some of my enthusiasm.

He looked at me with renewed suspicion. "How far have you read?"

Again, I was careful with my answer. "I'm ready to start the second to last chapter tomorrow."

He studied me some more. I was beginning to feel like some kind of foreign specimen the way he kept looking at me.

"Do you think you'll finish reading *The Magyke of the Elementes* tomorrow?"

"I do."

"Then perhaps the day after tomorrow we'll go over any questions you have about the book, before you start the next one."

I nodded. "Yes, that would be wonderful." In truth, I didn't have any pressing questions. More than anything, I wanted to figure out those things I didn't yet understand through experimentation. I was eager to attempt more of the practice lessons.

I would have to think of some questions to ask Marcelo. He didn't seem like the kind of man who appreciated disappointment.

~

The book finished by discussing the practical applications of elemental magic. Even as inexperienced as I was, I knew the uses of elemental magic must be far vaster than what the book suggested. It spoke of using fire to heat your food and to light a candle or a bonfire. But it didn't explain how to do anything beyond the predictable.

The Magyke of the Elementes taught that water magic could be used to fill pots for cooking, glasses for drinking, and bathtubs for bathing. It didn't say that the water for the bath could be heated, though I knew it could, by combining fire and water magic.

The book's exploration of earth and air was similarly limited. The magician could use earth magic to plane small plots of uneven land, to fill holes in the ground, and to clean houses by removing dust in one sweep of wizardry. There was no mention of making the earth shake or moving large sections of land, or of uniting earth and air magic to cause sand storms.

In its chapters dedicated to air wizardry, the book mentioned using air to blow out candles from across the room and to create a slight, localized breeze to cool you on a hot day. It didn't indicate that you could combine air and fire magic either to raise or lower the temperature. It didn't discuss the possibilities of employing air magic to create storms and then to change the atmospheric pressure to intensify them.

My imagination rapidly surpassed the limits of *The Magyke of the Elementes*. What would happen if a magician, witch, wizard, or sorcerer—I was still unclear about the differences in nomenclature—were fluent in the four basic elements of nature? Could a magician unite fire, water, earth, and air to create tempests of unimaginable intensity? Could he merge the four elements to sculpt matter and create that which hadn't existed before, simply by unifying components from nature that had the elements as their origins?

Could such a magician suck particles of earth from the ground and press them together to form a shape? Could he then imbue this figure with the water that hydrated and gave body, with the fire that gave personality, and with the air that gave breath to life forms?

I didn't know if these were questions I could ask Marcelo. Was this thinking he would sanction?

But then, perhaps it was more important for me to

117

discover what I was capable of than to seek Marcelo's approval.

I'd never thought of dismissing others' expectations of me before. I'd sought my parents' approval before I realized what approval was, and I'd never stopped.

Without doubt, I had crossed the line that demarcated the permissible and the forbidden with Father and Mother the moment I cracked open *The Magyke of the Elementes*. Since I'd already risked the discontent of my parents, it seemed that I should continue and risk that of Marcelo. What if that were the only way to discover who I really was?

So when Maggie helped me outside and set me up on a blanket in the midday sun to meet with Marcelo, I had already deliberated with myself for hours about the wisest course of action. When Marcelo sat down opposite me on the blanket, the part of me that had never felt so alive before reared its head and took over, disregarding my promises to myself that I would at least be cautious.

Marcelo and I looked toward the lake, allowing the sunshine to illuminate our faces. Blue highlights reflected throughout his black hair.

I looked at his face and wondered at his age. The way in which he carried himself had led me to assume that he was much older than me; his attitude was one of experience and wisdom. Yet looking at him now, I wasn't so sure anymore. He appeared youthful and vibrant, and that confused me.

Drawn to him and a radiance I hadn't seen in him before, I exclaimed, "I was able to do a little water magic."

I held my breath waiting for his response. This was not according to my plan.

He didn't say anything for the longest time, until I feared he might not say anything at all. I watched him run through a gamut of emotions that I interpreted as anger, frustration, fear, acceptance, and then, finally, curiosity.

"Why?" was all he said.

"I couldn't help myself. It's all so exciting. I want to try it all. But that's all I did. I waited for you to do the rest."

Sheepishly, I looked down, pretending to find the flowered print of my dress most interesting. "I read the entire book, every word." Although wearing clothing was a great relief after so many weeks limited to a nightgown, I didn't even see the tight little blue flowers I pretended to examine.

When I looked up again, Marcelo appeared resigned to what I think he'd known all along: He would have to teach me magic, more than he wanted.

Then, he shocked me.

He smiled, and I realized I still didn't really know him at all.

AN UNCOMMON PUPIL

e stayed outside for hours, until I couldn't withstand the chill of late winter any longer, though I tried. I didn't want my time with Marcelo to end.

Lake Creston wasn't Norland Manor, and so Maggie had left us alone in accordance with Marcelo's wishes. Mother would never have allowed me to be alone with a man, unattended by my lady's maid. But Mother wasn't here.

Magic had filled every crevice of time we carved out for ourselves in our partial seclusion. After my admissions, things went much better than I had anticipated. Marcelo showed me a side of himself I hadn't even suspected existed. There had been no hint of this vitality and enthusiasm in all his previous dealings with me.

Once he resigned himself to how things were—that I had disobeyed his limiting instructions and discovered the ability to control two elements on my own, and that now he would have to teach me a broader scope of magic—his demeanor transformed, as if a shell had cracked and fallen away.

I barely recognized the Marcelo in front of me. I watched him, following his every word, not wanting to miss a single one.

"The most important point of *The Magyke of the Elementes*, and the reason I wanted you to read it first, is to understand that our ability to control the elements comes from within us. It's because the four elements are part of us that we can do magic with them. It is, in fact, *natural* for us to work with the elements.

"I prefer to say that we work with the elements instead of 'manipulate' them as the book says. It's very important to give the elements the respect they deserve, and saying that we manipulate or control them doesn't do that. Each of the individual elements is immensely more powerful than us. We need to remember that and always show respect in our words and actions.

"We can work with the elements because they allow it. That's the only reason. Should we command them to work with us when they don't want to..." Marcelo stopped to shudder. "Well, I don't know exactly what would happen as I've never done it before, but I'm certain that it would be ugly and, undoubtedly, it would be dark. And we *never* want to meddle with dark magic." He stared deep into my eyes. "*Never.*"

"I understand." I wanted to ask what would happen if I did try dark magic, but the look on his face was forbidding.

He turned to look at the lake, where he distracted himself with a thought or a memory. Then he turned back toward me. "Not only do the elements live within us, but they're in our environment as well. That's why the situation is already ideal for transitioning between the elemental in us to the elemental that surrounds us."

"That makes a lot of sense." I gathered enough courage to add, "It was easy for me to do the first exercise with water in the book. It was as if it were all set up for me, just waiting for me to complete the steps to do it."

"Yes, well, what you did isn't common. It's not common at all." The look on his face implied that this was not a good thing.

"What do you mean?"

"It usually takes novice pupils at least a year of study, sometimes several years, before they're able to perform even one exercise. They must first understand all the concepts that are woven into the art of magic before they figure out how to relate to it. Somehow, you've been able to circumvent all this study. You understood fire and water without any instruction or fundamental knowledge about them. That's very rare."

"How long did it take you to be able to do magic?"

My question shut him down. The Marcelo I had enjoyed for hours withdrew again. "My past is not your concern. I'm here to teach you what I must to keep you safe, and then my responsibility to the Count of Norland will be complete. We're finished for the day. I'll fetch Maggie to help you inside."

I watched him retreat, with indignant, heavy footsteps, to the lake house.

Instead of making me cower, his anger made me curious. What was there in his past that made him so defensive?

SURRENDER TO SOMETHING BIG

*M*arcelo didn't bring me a new book the next morning as I expected he would, nor did he bring it to me the next day. He didn't come to see me at all. Instead, he instructed Maggie to ensure my wounds were still healing well.

When he didn't come the third day, a wave of my own anger surged. What had I done that was so wrong that he should ignore me like this?

He was in the house, locked in his chambers. He must eat and drink at some point. But if he came out for food or water, neither Maggie nor I noticed him.

All I had done was show a natural curiosity about that which he was most passionate. He should be happy to have such an eager pupil. But instead, he was punishing me. How terrible could his past possibly be that he would castigate me just for asking about his beginnings in magic?

And why was it so difficult for him to accept that he was going to have to teach me? Was it because I was a girl?

124

My entire life, my parents had seen me as less because I was a girl. I hoped Marcelo would have more sense than that.

My anger mounted as I considered all the righteous reasons for it. But as agitated as I was becoming about what I interpreted as Marcelo's unjust treatment, I forgot about it in an instant.

Something was happening. Something big.

I didn't know what it was, and it scared me at first.

Then I surrendered to it. Since I didn't understand it and there was little I could do anyway, I let curiosity win over my fear.

A flash of intense, searing heat that made me flush but didn't burn me raced across my skin. It radiated across all points of my body at once. It was overpowering and made me feel faint. I leaned back against the pillows and clinched my eyes closed. I found it difficult to breathe.

I began to panic again and that made me hyperventilate. But hyperventilating forced me to calm down—I had no choice if I wanted to pull in the air my body desperately needed.

I was uncomfortable beyond belief, and I still had no explanation for what was happening or why it had begun without warning. I didn't even remember why I'd been angry. All I wanted was for the sensation to pass.

The flashes of heat continued to radiate out from my center until they covered all parts of my body, ending with my extremities, where they finally dissipated.

But by then, a new wave was on its way.

Over and again, the searing heat pulsed from my center.

Every muscle in my body was clenched against it. My body fought to repel the discomfort.

It couldn't.

Then, it was over.

Just as the sensations had begun without warning, so they ended.

I lay limp against the bed as if I had no bones. The exertion had drained me of any thought I might have had.

I closed my eyes and focused on breathing. I savored my chest's steady rise and fall as my breath normalized.

I wouldn't realize what had happened to me until later.

THE INCREDIBLE, THE UNLIKELY,
AND THE NEARLY IMPOSSIBLE

I remained without moving, a leg draped off the side of the bed, for what seemed like forever. I may have fallen asleep. I didn't know. I couldn't think. I didn't understand.

When I finally did open my eyes, I watched the leaves on the oak tree outside my window sparkle as they swayed in the breeze for so long that time stole away like an unnoticed stranger.

Eventually, Maggie entered the room to check on me. The moment her foot crossed the threshold she broke into a run.

"Clara! Clara! Are you all right?" she yelled at me, even though she was at my bedside.

I didn't answer at first. Once my mind recovered from the experience, it remained elsewhere, firmly entrenched in a world of not knowing or caring.

"Clara. Oh no." Maggie sounded like she was about to cry.

I mumbled. "I'll be fine. I think. I don't know."

I didn't convince Maggie, with good reason, and she spun on her heel and ran back out of the room. I heard her through the open doorway, running down hallways and then pounding at Marcelo's door.

He said nothing, but I heard Maggie. "Come quick. Something isn't right with Clara."

Then two sets of footsteps thundered down the halls, and I still didn't understand anything about anything. The leaves continued to flutter in the wind that I imagined blew outside my closed window.

My eyes closed against my will, and I felt as if the wind were blowing on my skin after all. Every bit of me felt cool, completely recovered from the intense heat. The breeze blew another time, gently, and my skin exulted.

Maggie reached me again, this time with Marcelo in tow. He swept his gaze furiously across my prostrate form, my left leg still draped off the bed, dangling, as I guessed my whole body would if the bed weren't supporting it.

As if I were very far away, I watched deep concern creep across Marcelo's face.

Then his eyes narrowed.

He grabbed at my arm in a brutish movement. And in so doing, he substantiated the incredible, the unlikely, and the nearly impossible.

Hastily, he untied the ribbon that encircled the cuff of my sleeve. He pushed my sleeve up.

Maggie gasped.

Marcelo said and did nothing.

They both stared.

My skin was completely healed.

CURIOUS, EXCITING, AND FRIGHTENING THINGS

*B*y that same night, the fog had cleared from my mind, and I felt myself again. I answered every one of Marcelo's questions—I could have refused to answer his questions as he'd ignored mine, but I didn't. I told him everything I knew, which wasn't much.

I felt as if I were reliving the days after my first experiences with fire all over again. Marcelo camped out in my room that night and the next day, pacing furiously, and then consulting his books with just as much fervor. This time he did talk to me, although not often and not much. Still, it was an improvement from the previous times.

At one point, he exited my room, and I heard him walk in his long strides toward his own chambers. Though my skin was now healed as if the burns had never happened, yesterday's occurrence had exhausted me, and I had little energy to move from the bed. I relied on my hearing to satiate my curiosity.

Marcelo went into his rooms, was in them for maybe ten minutes, and then came out again. He gave Maggie a letter to dispatch to Father right away. I followed the sound of Maggie's footsteps as she left the lake house and headed toward the stables, no doubt looking for Thomas. He could go into town and find the courier they had used before.

I was surprised to find that I didn't really care what the letter said. A part of me realized how important any communication between Marcelo and Father was. There was still time, though not much—mere days—for Father to meet the Count of Chester's deadline.

My life had become so different from anything I'd known before that I couldn't even put myself in the right frame of mind to consider the effects of their missives. There were more pressing things happening in my life— much more curious, exciting, and frightening things.

In the world of limitless possibilities I'd discovered, my menacing fiancé seemed inconsequential. It was as if I'd laid a puzzle out within my mind, and Winston was an unimportant, extraneous piece that didn't belong to the puzzle. This was the case with my parents and my sisters too, though not with Gertrude. I felt just as bonded to Gertrude as ever, and I knew she still played an important part in my life.

By the time Marcelo returned to my room, I was able to look at his tousled hair and distracted expression affectionately. There was much more to explore in the world of magic, and Marcelo was the one who would teach me.

Fate had aligned it so.

The searing heat on my skin hadn't burned me this time.

It had healed me. I was venturing into tendencies in magic that weren't contained by Marcelo's books or experience.

FATE'S DETERMINATIONS

I was outside by myself. Finally. The sun shone extra brightly, and it seemed like all of nature cooperated to make my first venture outdoors alone in almost two months idyllic. Birds chirped and sang.

A day like today was not one to be wasted on fears or worries. I entertained no thoughts of Winston, my parents, Marcelo, or even magic. My mind was blissfully empty of distractions. I watched the sunlight sparkle across the lake's surface. Occasional fish jumped out of the water, landing with a splash. I noticed the ripples that encircled their landing dissipate until they vanished.

I felt more myself than before the fever. It was a happy day. I just wished Gertrude were here to share it with me.

I leaned back against the blanket Maggie had spread out for me. It was soft and warm. Although it would horrify her if she saw me, I sat up to unlace my shoes. I took them off, rolled down my half hose, and put my feet on the grass.

Almost without thinking, my hands shot to my back.

They fumbled with the intricate lacing of my bodice. It was hard to breathe with this thing on.

Now that I had fully healed from the fever and my skin had recovered from its burns, Maggie insisted I wear a bodice. Like Mother, she said that a lady had to. The leniency she gave my hair didn't extend to my corset.

Finally, I loosened it. I breathed fully, tasting crisp, fresh air. I leaned back onto the blanket again.

The sun dipped behind a cloud. The lake ceased its glittering, just for a few moments, making what would happen next all the more apparent.

Marcelo watched me from the bay window in his chambers, though he didn't tell me that until later. It was thanks to this silent vigil that he finally decided to teach me as much as I was capable of learning.

Fate determined my life for me, and it took me far away from everything I knew during my first sixteen years at Norland Manor.

AN ALL-CONSUMING COMMITMENT

 here were only four days left before the Count
of Chester's deadline. Since my parents hadn't
requested my return to Norland Manor (at least not that I
was aware of), I happily concluded that they still believed
me too ill to marry. I desperately clung to that assumption.

Marcelo was the only one in direct communication with
my parents. I'd asked him for details of his arrangement
with them as many times as I dared, but he shut me down
on every occasion.

When the direct approach didn't work, I attempted
discrete fishing expeditions that probably weren't as
discrete as I thought and yielded no success regardless.
Finally, I resorted to assigning Maggie the difficult—and
eventually fruitless task—of wrangling information out of
Marcelo. We quickly learned that the brooding wizard was
not one easily wrangled. I gave up soon thereafter.

I resigned myself to accept the unspoken agreement that

he obviously believed we had. He would take care of things as he saw fit, and I just had to trust him.

I understand now that he intended it to be one of my first lessons in the study of magic. In order to explore my full capacity, I had to trust my teacher.

So as Marcelo and I walked the lakeshore, the soles of my feet happily allowing it, I forced myself to put Winston and my parents far from my thoughts and focused on what the man next to me was saying.

"The study of magic requires a lot of effort."

I was already nodding vigorously, trying to convey my enthusiastic readiness to learn magic.

"Don't be so quick to agree. This is a very serious matter," he said. Then he laughed.

"You went from looking excited to somber in a second. It was humorous," he said, smiling out at the lake. When he turned back toward me, he was all business again.

"If you agree to study magic with me, it'll be a very big commitment. I'll require that magic and our studies become your complete focus. There can be no distractions."

I waited to express my agreement now. I knew there was still more.

"It'll be intense. The practice of magic will bring things up in you. You'll have to deal with these healing and growing issues on your own. That'll be your responsibility, and you must do this inner work or you'll be incapable of becoming the magician you could be. Interacting with elemental magic as profoundly as you will is a perilous venture if you aren't a stable individual. Do you understand how important this factor is?"

I nodded solemnly.

"I won't be your counselor or your friend. I'm your teacher. You deal with your emotions on your own. I won't lend an ear for your feelings. We're perfectly clear on this?"

"Yes."

"The magic I teach you will be all-consuming. It's the only proper way to learn magic. It's how I learned, and it's how my teacher learned, and it's the same way his teacher did as well."

I waited to see if he would reveal more about his beginnings in magic, but it was futile.

"If you don't put in the effort I require of you—no, that *magic* requires of you—I'll quit you."

Marcelo revisited the brusqueness of our past interactions, and I stiffened.

"I'm doing what I feel led to do. I've come to believe that you were put in my path purposefully and that it's my responsibility to teach you to harness your natural gifts and to use them responsibly. But if you don't do your part, I'll consider myself freed of this contract."

"I understand. I'm ready to do what you ask of me."

"Are you sure you know what you're getting into?"

"Of course I don't know what I'm getting into. How could I? But, like you, likely more than you, I don't feel as if I have a real choice. This is my path. I may be young, but I know my own mind. This is what has lined up for me, and there's a good reason for it. I'm ready, for whatever it is. And I promise that I'll always do my best and give my greatest effort."

Marcelo's gaze was startlingly intense. His blue eyes

blazed. "Yes, I suppose that's all you can do. Very well. Let's begin then."

"When do we start?"

"Now. I've already planned out your first lesson."

However, Marcelo hadn't quite closed the front door to the lake house behind us when he opened it again.

THE THREAT OF A LIFE OF
UNPLEASANTNESS

*T*he thundering sound of galloping hooves barreled our way. My heart pumped in my chest. What could it be? The rider showed no signs of slowing as he raced down the drive.

The rider still hadn't slowed when I saw that it was a she and not a he after all. The realization made my heart beat even faster. Why would Maggie be riding a horse like a man? And whose horse was she riding?

Now that I was better, Maggie had taken to going into town some days instead of sending Thomas. But I'd seen her when she left this morning. She'd left on foot.

Maggie skidded to a halt directly by the front door, bathing us in a cloud of dust that would have otherwise been intolerable. She jumped down from the horse and stood in the swirl of dirt.

"Winston, the second son of the House of Chester, and several of his men are in town. He found out that Clara's been staying with a man with a questionable reputation." She spit the words out as quickly as she could. There was no time for apologetic looks. Marcelo was well aware of the reputation that preceded him and all magicians.

"If Clara doesn't prove that she can't marry him because she's sick, he'll fetch her away with him."

My eyes widened in alarm. I turned to snap accusingly at Marcelo. "Did you know about this?"

"Of course I didn't," he snapped back. "How far behind you are they, Maggie?"

"Not far. They should be here in under an hour. Maybe sooner."

"Maggie, will you be okay to stay behind?"

"Yes, Sir."

"You know they may be violent."

"Yes, Sir, I do. I'll say that I know nothing and that you two just took off."

We were all quiet for a moment. Even though I'd led a relatively sheltered life, I knew what sires and their men were capable of. Marcelo and Maggie knew it even better than I did.

"Maggie, you don't have to do this," I said. "You could be hurt."

"I'll be all right, whatever it is, Milady. This is my duty. If he finds you here—" Maggie couldn't finish. "Well, let's just say that he made it overly clear that he wouldn't be a gentleman about it. He wasn't shy in his descriptions of what he'd do to you." Maggie looked down with these last words, affording me the dignity that Winston had not.

Whatever Winston would do to me would only be the beginning of a lifetime of unpleasantness at his side.

"Is Thomas here?" Marcelo asked.

"I believe so, Sir."

"Go fetch him right away. Tell him to prepare my horse immediately. And tell him to bring anything he has to defend you and meet us in the house. Tell him to be as quick as he can."

Maggie was already in motion. I watched her run toward the stables with a deep sadness in my heart.

Marcelo yanked me by my arm inside the house.

ESCAPING REALITY

*M*arcelo had ordered me to gather only the essentials and throw them in a bag. But this was not an easy request for a young woman of the nobility. I had so many extraneous things and garments that in the end I couldn't decide what was important and what wasn't.

My mind was racing ahead of itself in anguish and concern for Maggie so that I couldn't concentrate. In the end, I grabbed only two dresses and my hair and tooth-brush, threw them in my small leather bag, and closed it up. I pulled on my winter coat, wrapped a scarf around my throat, and went to find Marcelo.

But I didn't need to find him. He found me. In fact, he ran right into me, dropping his two bags. He didn't hesitate or take time to recover from the impact. He snatched his bags up in one hand, grabbed me with the other, and ushered us out the back door, toward the stables.

He half pushed me as I kept looking over my shoulder. I

wanted to say goodbye to Maggie. I hadn't thought I wouldn't get the chance to hug my friend before we left.

I felt responsible for her well-being. Winston was coming for me. If I'd accepted my parents' wedding arrangements, Maggie wouldn't be in harm's way.

"Move it, Clara. There's no time for farewells," Marcelo said, correctly interpreting my backward glances. As if to make his point, the sound of horses reached us. It wasn't loud yet, but the ground beneath us vibrated. They would be upon us before we could get away without being seen.

Marcelo didn't have to tell me what the sounds meant or insist on the renewed urgency of our departure. I broke into a run before he did.

"Sir, I prepared your horse and another for the lady as ya wish," Thomas yelled out. He was standing at the ready, holding two horses by their bridals at the stable entrance. They were saddled to ride.

Marcelo flicked an efficient glance at me while we took the last running steps to reach Thomas. "Can you ride?"

"Of course I can."

"Do you ride well?"

"Very."

Winston and his men were racing down the drive now. The driveway was lengthy, but it wouldn't be long before they reached us.

Marcelo started to hook one of his bags on the side of the saddle but then thought better of it. They were loaded with his books and would slow us down.

"Leave your bag," Marcelo told me.

I dropped it immediately.

"I'll send word of where you can send them," Marcelo told Thomas.

"Go now, Sir" Thomas said. "They're already here."

With a glance at me, Marcelo set his horse at a trot. We couldn't race right past Winston and his troop, not with Maggie and Thomas remaining behind.

I edged my horse right next to Marcelo's. Whatever he did, I'd imitate, and I had the feeling whatever he did would be sudden and unexpected. I was alert, all my senses heightened by threat and fear.

Maggie was at the lake house's front door. I got to say goodbye to her after all, even though it was silent. She met my eyes, and we said everything in that look and my sad smile.

Then she turned toward the approaching riders. My eyes burned at the courage and selflessness I witnessed in her.

I looked toward the riders as well. Righteous anger and determination swelled within me, and Marcelo snuck a wary glance at me. Under his breath, he whispered sternly, "Control yourself. No powers."

I understood Marcelo's clipped message. I shouldn't allow Winston or his men to see what I was capable of. It was beyond dangerous. If evidence of witchcraft caused hysteria among even the most rational of townspeople, it certainly would provoke a significant reaction in Winston.

Even though I knew relatively little about him, I knew to be vigilant. Bullies sought to exploit the disadvantages of others. Winston would certainly use the threat of exposing my magic to coerce me into submitting to his will. And if he ever disclosed my secret, there was only one possible outcome for me: the town pyre or submersion in the lake. With my red hair, I'd likely be subjected to the same fate as the unfortunate baker's daughter.

I realized how important it was that I keep my powers hidden. Regardless, this was a most difficult demand. I didn't yet know how to control my powers.

Like a tickle in your throat, which couldn't become a cough, or a sneeze building that couldn't be released, I squirmed, uncomfortable in my own skin. I didn't know what would happen, and I didn't know how to stop or direct whatever might. I just knew I was getting angry, and that worried me.

Marcelo guided his horse over to where Maggie stood. I followed.

Winston stopped in front of us all.

At first, I was confused. Winston looked like Samuel, and Samuel was kind. I hadn't met Winston. I'd based all my fears on Samuel's impressions of his brother.

Perhaps I'd been wrong to think so poorly of him. A flutter of hope passed through me.

But that hope flew away faster than a startled finch.

"So you're the wench my parents think worthy of marrying me?" His voice had a pitch to it that didn't quite fit the body. He was a young man of average size, but his voice was that of an entitled boy.

I was afraid to speak. We still didn't know exactly what Winston had planned for this meeting. I couldn't think of anything to say that wouldn't escalate the conflict. I remained silent.

Apparently Winston's remark had the same effect on Marcelo as it did on me, because the vein on the right side of his neck was bulging.

"That's not how a lady should be addressed, and I won't allow such disrespect to her honor to take place in my presence."

"Oh, you're going to defend her honor, are you?" Winston's men, used to his bullying taunts, laughed loudly. Half the men laughed because they feared Winston; the other half laughed because they were just as foul as him.

The laughter died down and all that remained was a very important silence. It made Marcelo's response sound as strong as it was meant to be.

"Yes, I am."

Those of the men who were as horrible as their master chuckled. Those who rode along out of obligation noticed the power in Marcelo's statement and backed away from Winston. Their movement wasn't visible, it was only energetic, but I felt it, and I'm certain Marcelo did too.

Marcelo nudged his horse a step closer to Winston. This time I didn't follow. "What are your intentions here today?"

"My intentions?" Winston threw his head back and laughed. It was a terrible sound. Involuntarily, a shudder ran through me. That my parents would consider marrying me away to a man such as this was unthinkable. Yet that's the way it was: reality.

This reality had short, groomed blonde hair, unruffled by riding. His smile was big and clean. He sat upright on his horse, his attire, impeccable.

But his eyes leached iniquity. It was an awful image to

face. I placed all my hope in Marcelo, that it would not become a reality I'd have to face every day for the rest of my life.

"My intentions are to take my future wife—who's clearly in well enough health to marry—away from here. She'll ride with us to Chester, where we'll marry as planned."

"That's not going to happen," Marcelo said in a voice that was too calm.

"How dare you! It's my right. The Count of Norland has made an agreement with my father, the Count of Chester, that this girl is to marry me. Therefore, she's mine, and I can do with her as I wish. This is in no way your concern. Now, step away."

"No."

"Excuse me? I must have misheard you, because no one speaks to me that way."

"I just did."

Winston drew his sword, and half his men followed suit. They took one step forward. The other half of Winston's men stayed where they were, physically distancing themselves from Winston without having moved at all.

I noticed for the first time that Marcelo carried a sword at his side. However, he didn't move to draw it.

"I'm going to tell you what's going to happen. You and your men are going to sheathe your swords, and you're going to turn around and return to Chester, or wherever it is you came from. You're going to leave without harming anyone. No one here has done anything to harm you."

"Well, let me tell you all the ways in which you're mistaken. Someone here has harmed me. This wench has.

She's my property, and it's my right to have her. And you're harming me by interfering with what's rightfully mine. I suppose the servants haven't harmed me, though this one here could be good for a little fun. I like the dark and swarthy look."

Some cackles rose from the men nearest him, and one shouted out, "He likes all the looks, don't he?"

I looked at Maggie. She appeared terrified.

I thought I might vomit, and I began to tremble involuntarily. Immediately, I tried to squelch the shuddering. But it didn't make a difference. I couldn't stop the violent shaking; it was fear manifesting. I just hoped Winston or his men wouldn't notice.

"You'll do as I say and retreat peacefully, leaving everyone unharmed. Or I'll make you."

I noticed Thomas had moved closer to us. He stood leaning on a shovel. I didn't think he brought the shovel because he was planning on digging.

"Oh yeah? And how do you plan on doing that?" Laughter hung on Winston's face.

Now Marcelo drew his sword. The telltale *shliiing* pierced Winston's laughter. He paused, but just for a moment. "You think a sword scares me?"

"No. But mine should scare you."

A flicker of doubt crossed even the hardiest of Winston's companions, but Winston remained unaffected. I had no idea how Marcelo, with his one sword, would defeat a dozen armed men.

But I also knew what Winston apparently didn't: Marcelo was a wizard.

Maggie and I watched Marcelo closely. We had no idea of Marcelo's capabilities, and we didn't want to miss whatever came next.

"Maggie and Thomas, go inside the house and bolt the doors. These men won't be bothering you any longer."

Maggie looked regretful that she would miss the show, but she didn't hesitate in complying. I heard Thomas throwing the bolts and Maggie pulling the shutters shut.

Marcelo looked at Winston's companions. "You are free to go, as long as you cause no harm here. I have no quarrel with any of you."

None of them moved. They couldn't decide if they were more afraid of Marcelo or Winston.

To Winston, Marcelo said, "You too can leave unharmed if you leave right now. But you can never bother Lady Clara again. Forget her."

Winston moved closer to us. He lunged at Marcelo, sword first. Marcelo deflected Winston's sword. Then he led his horse away from me, effectively drawing Winston away with him.

I edged farther away, to the side of Winston and his troop, pointing my horse toward the open driveway beyond them. I knew Marcelo and I might need to make an escape. We were vastly outnumbered, and Winston and the men behind him gave off the impression that they'd killed many times before. They emanated a general disregard for the life and well-being of others.

Despite Marcelo's admirable display of bravado, I didn't know how skilled he was with a sword, or if he could defend us through the use of magic. There was an inherent danger in using magic around people such as these. The effects of Marcelo's actions could be long lasting.

But I soon realized there was nothing to fear. Marcelo understood the consequences of his choices better than I did.

As he pushed Winston's sword back, Winston's horse reared. Winston appeared to be as surprised as I was, but Marcelo didn't look surprised at all.

It was then that I looked at Marcelo's face more closely and discovered the same look he had when he was attempting to resolve a problem. I recognized the telltale signs that his mind was moving rapidly, solving the present problem through a quick consideration of possible solutions.

His head pointed forward toward Winston, but his eyes only vaguely watched him.

That was the first time I considered that Marcelo might be truly brilliant.

My shivering had subsided some, but not all the way. Winston and his men would have no trouble hurting me or anyone I cared about.

Marcelo remained calm and in control. The lives of three people and the responsibility of safe escape landed on him. He didn't shirk from the weight of it.

And as Winston's horse reared again, I knew this had to be Marcelo's magic. I didn't know how Marcelo was affecting the horse, but it was the only reasonable explanation. Horses like these, trained in a house of nobility, were reliable and predictable.

If the Court at Chester was anything like the Court at

Norland, I knew it was likely that Winston had chosen the horse himself and been a part of his horse's training. Winston and his horse would have grown very comfortable with each other before the horse would accompany him on scouting expeditions. The nobility didn't take chances with its steeds.

The astonishment on Winston's face confirmed my suspicions. His horse didn't usually act like this.

"Whoa, boy. Whoa, Warrior. Whoa. Whoa. It's all right, boy." Winston rubbed his hand along Warrior's neck while the horse puffed hot air. He held on to Warrior's harness with the other hand.

It was a miracle that Warrior hadn't thrown him the two times he reared. Winston was unprepared for the unexpected behavior and survived it only because his instincts made him clutch the horse's body with his legs.

"It's all right, boy. Shhh. Shhh." Winston actually sounded nice when he spoke to his horse.

Warrior began to calm at his master's soothing.

But that was not part of Marcelo's plan. There were eleven men in Winston's company, and now eleven horses reared in a racket of whinnies and snorts.

The men were assembled close to one another. Their horses fought for space. They reared almost on top of one another until their masters pulled them back.

The banded group dispersed by necessity.

Two of the horses threw their riders before galloping up the drive, disappearing quickly. The men lay on the ground for only a moment before crawling out of the way of crashing hooves.

The remaining horses continued their attempts to throw their masters. They bucked and reared, and I knew more men would fall to the ground shortly.

Like the men, the chaos had temporarily consumed my attention. Now I remembered Marcelo and turned to find him. He wasn't facing the scene of thrashing horses. He faced the lake house.

Then, he turned to find me.

He discovered me already looking at him and gave me a subtle nod.

I set my horse in motion. Marcelo was on my heels.

We charged up the drive as fast as our horses could carry us.

I looked behind me several times, but the scene was the same: riders struggling with their horses and men holding their sides or limbs in pain from nasty falls.

Marcelo pulled up beside me.

"What about Maggie and Thomas?" I called over the drumming of hooves.

"They'll be safe. I cast a spell. Winston and his band won't be able to enter, disturb, or set fire to the house."

A rush of relief came with Marcelo's answer. I'd worried that Winston would get frustrated if he couldn't enter the house and try to burn Maggie and Thomas alive inside it.

"Thank you, Marcelo." I very much meant it.

THE BUSINESS OF CRUEL FATES

We rode hard until our horses and I grew tired. Once we left Winston and his men behind, the trembling finally subsided. The fear and tension left exhaustion in its place. I felt like a rag doll in the saddle. I asked for a break.

"Not yet," Marcelo said over our continued galloping.

"Why not? We've been riding without pause for hours. Surely we've lost Winston and his men by now."

"Winston will begin looking for us as soon as he's able to reassemble. We must be prudent in our actions. We'll stop when we find the two horses."

"Winston's horses? The horses that ran away?" I was confused. We'd traveled a great distance from Lake Creston already. The horses could be anywhere. But I didn't say anything more.

I followed Marcelo's lead wordlessly, until my trust was rewarded. Marcelo slowed his horse to a trot and edged to the side of the road. He was looking for something. When he found it, he led me down a path of trampled grasses. Tree branches reached toward me, snaring my dress and adorning my loose hair with twigs.

We reached a small clearing, and there were the two runaway horses. They looked at us, as if they had expected us.

"I can't believe it," I said under my breath.

Marcelo chuckled.

"What's so funny?"

"You have inexplicable experiences with fire and water, yet you can't believe that I, a magician, could locate two horses that ran away because I caused them to?"

Still, I was amazed. I'd been around horses a lot, and I knew that horses that ran from their masters usually didn't want to return to domestication.

Despite my disbelief, these horses stood still while Marcelo approached them. Their reins hung loose, trailing against the ground, and Marcelo swept up the reins of the chestnut horse and ran his hand along the length of his neck. The horse let him. Marcelo whispered to the horse, but I couldn't make out what he said.

"How did you do it? Are you a horse charmer?" I'd never met a horse charmer before, or an animal charmer of any sort, but I'd heard rumors of them.

Marcelo was about to dismiss my question, as was his habit, but he was supposed to be teaching me now. After a reluctant sigh, he answered. "When the horses escaped, I was able to put a marker on them, a sort of magical tag, one that only I could see. Once we left, I honed in on that tag and followed it here."

"That's incredible." I'd never heard of such a thing! The idea of being able to do something like what Marcelo had done opened a world of possibilities I'd never considered. "Will I be able to learn to do that?"

"I imagine you will."

"How did you do it? Was it a spell or something?" Even after reading *The Magyke of the Elementes*, I still wasn't clear on how a wizard performed magic. The book didn't address many of the details, and it didn't address any of the ways in which I had accidentally done magic.

He looked at me thoughtfully. "I did perform a spell."

"I didn't hear you say anything. Did you say the spell out loud?"

"I did, though I spoke softly. I couldn't allow Winston to realize what was going on."

I thought I'd observed Marcelo closely through the extent of the skirmish. I realized now I would have to pay closer attention to the minute details if I was to learn exactly how he executed his brand of magic.

"I don't have the feeling that you'll be doing magic through spells," he said, as if he'd read my mind.

"How will I do magic if I won't be using spells?"

"The same way you've already done magic." Then he turned his attention to the other horse.

I had so much to learn. I didn't even understand what I'd already done. I blew my hair out of my eyes in a frustrated huff, tried to straighten my dress out, and then dismounted. I'd ridden like a man in a man's saddle. There was no time for prudence or etiquette; a woman's sidesaddle wouldn't have done. We never would have been able to move as fast as we did.

Once my feet hit the ground, my entire body screamed for one moment, and then all that remained were sore thighs and buttocks. I would be hurting for days. I limped gingerly over to Marcelo and petted the chestnut horse.

"What are we going to do now? Are you taking me to Norland?"

Marcelo shook his head. "I fear that if I take you to Norland, your father will hand you over to Winston. From his correspondence, he sounds like a severe man."

He searched my eyes and found the confirmation he was looking for.

Unlike Marcelo, Father was outspoken about his opinions, especially when it came to those regarding my sisters and me. He would have emphasized my duty as a future wife and the advantages my proposed union could afford our family. I was expected to do as he told me; the interests of the family were to come before my own. Father was unyielding in most aspects of life, and he most especially was when it concerned my duty.

He would have inquired about my health only to determine whether I could meet the Count of Chester's deadline. His letters to Marcelo would have omitted any evidence of parental affection. Affection was what governesses were for.

I thought I saw a flicker of compassion reveal itself beneath Marcelo's otherwise tempestuous façade.

"Then where will we go?"

"I haven't figured that part out yet. Do you have any ideas?"

"No."

The temptation of allowing Marcelo to whisk me away somewhere that I could be free from the imminent threat of marriage was strong. But I understood how big of a risk he would be taking in helping me, even if he didn't. If Father ever found out that Marcelo was purposefully interfering with my marriage to Winston, Father wouldn't stop until he destroyed Marcelo.

I had seen Father do it before. He'd crushed those that opposed him, using the full arsenal of attack available to a member of the nobility: scandal, gossip, accusations of betrayal, and favors.

Devastating Marcelo would be too easy. All Father would have to do was reveal Marcelo's propensities for magic to the people of whatever town he happened to be in at the time, and Marcelo would be lucky to escape with his life.

I didn't want to say what I was beginning to think I should say. I really, really didn't.

But I felt that I had to.

As unfortunate as my life circumstances were, they were not Marcelo's fault, and it wasn't his obligation to extricate me from them. The risk to his well-being was too great to ask it of a man I barely knew.

Still, a part of me desperately wanted to accept his help.

I said it before I could change my mind. "Marcelo, perhaps you should take me to Norland."

Marcelo's eyes flashed surprise and confusion. "Do you want to marry Winston?"

"No! Of course not. But I don't see how this will work

out. You can't just *take* me. Even if you and I know you saved me, my father won't see it that way. He'll persecute you until you return me. And after, he'll punish you for your actions. He won't stop until he destroys you."

"He seems like the kind of man who would do as you say."

Such a deep sadness plunged through my heart then that I could barely speak. The horse I was touching felt it and nuzzled against my hand.

"I can't ask you to forfeit your life to save me from what seems to be my inevitable fate."

"And what fate is that exactly? I thought you said fate had brought magic into your life."

"Maybe I was wrong. I see no way out of this that doesn't end badly for you. I was born a woman, and this seems to be the fate of women."

I gulped, finding the courage to continue. "Please. Take me to Norland. We can tell my father that you saved me from Winston's violent aggressions and that you thought it best to bring me to Norland. He won't hold that against you, and you'll be free to go."

"And you? You'll marry Winston? You saw what he was like back at the lake house. I think it safe to say that he'll beat you if you marry." Marcelo looked me in the eye to make sure I understood what he meant, "And worse."

I was still naïve and innocent in many ways of the world, but I did have some idea of how bad it could get when a man wanted to force himself upon a woman. I would be obligated to beget him children. That would be a requisite part of any marriage contract. I would certainly not be the first, nor the last, girl forced to marry a man she despised and then further obligated to bed him.

"Perhaps it won't be as bad as we think." Not a single part of me believed this lie. It was no surprise that I didn't convince Marcelo either.

"I can't let you do that. I can't let you marry him."

"Marcelo, it isn't you that's making me. It's my parents. *I* can't let *you* sacrifice your life for mine. It might not keep me from this cruel sentence anyway. My father is powerful. He has many resources at his disposal. And he isn't a kind man."

The truth of my life as I'd just described it left me dejected.

"Clara, look at me."

I dragged my eyes up from the ground to meet his, but I couldn't hold his gaze. He reached over and took my chin. He tilted my head up until my eyes stared into his. "I can't let you do this. I can't take you back there."

I started to protest, but he stopped me.

"I'm going to tell you a story that I don't tell many people. Only because I think it will help you understand why I have to help you."

~

"*Your* assumptions about me are correct. I was born into a noble line. My father is the Count of Bundry, just to the north, outside the borders of this country. It is part of no country. There have been a few attempts to take Bundry over the centuries, all unsuccessful. The land almost defends itself. Bundry is all rocky cliffs and overhangs, and it's bitterly cold in the winter. The sea beats at the rocks below relentlessly, whipping up an icy wind that rises up into the town.

"That wind can freeze a person on contact. I saw it happen once. An old woman who wasn't right in the head anymore took a walk along the city walls, overlooking the sea. She wore no coat or shoes though it was mid-winter. Well, that wind froze her standing upright."

A sympathy shiver ran through me even though it wasn't that cold; the sun still heated the day.

"As you can imagine, living in Bundry had its challenges, and my father is lord of it all. We have many things in common, you and I."

We did?

"Like you, I had an older brother who died when he was a boy."

Had I told him about Charles? I couldn't remember.

"He died when he was fourteen, when he'd already shown my parents what an exceptional heir he was. He did everything the way they wanted, and they put him on a pedestal. He was uncompromising, like my father, who said it would serve him well for when he ruled over Bundry. My brother died when I was seven, leaving me memories of him that are full of unkindness. He ridiculed my sister and me, and he hit us a lot. He believed mercy to be a weakness, and he didn't offer either of us any, even though my sister was a girl and I was much younger than him."

At the mention of his sister, a dreadful feeling spread

through my stomach. I waited for the rest of the story, hoping my suspicions were wrong.

"My sister was six years older than me, yet even when I was little, I tried to protect her. My father did nothing to intervene with my brother's behavior toward us. I wonder if he may have even privately congratulated him for it. My father was a firm believer in ruling with an iron hand. It was the only way to maintain order, he'd say.

"My father was stern with my mother as well. She was a meek woman who did her duty just like any of the servants. She was there to do my father's bidding, and she wouldn't intervene with my father or brother to protect her other two children. She never did anything that would upset my father.

"When my brother died from disease, my father became enraged and meaner than ever, and most of that rage landed on me. I would clearly be a disappointment, but it was my duty to do everything that I could to become like my brother. Meanwhile, it was my nightmare to be anything like him. I was secretly relieved that he'd died. And even though she never said it, I know my sister was too.

"Things got even uglier in our household. My father began to beat me, sure that he could force me into submission. It only made me more resolute: I wouldn't become a monster like them.

"When his violence didn't work on me, he threatened to beat my sister until I agreed to behave as he wished." Marcelo looked down now, as if ashamed. "I couldn't allow him to beat her, so I relented. I pretended to be like my

brother. My father even started calling me Patrice sometimes, my brother's name.

"Then my father decided it was time to marry my sister
away. She and I both wished so hard that he might choose a
kind man. After the home we lived in, there was a good
chance that wherever she went would be better than there.

"But it wasn't. My sister, Clarissa, was married to a man
much her senior. One who was very wealthy. Very powerful. He had… ways of getting people to do as he wanted.

"He'd already been married twice before. Both of his
past wives had died from accidents within the estate.
Clarissa and I knew what that might mean, but we
continued to hope for the best. She was only fourteen and I
was eight. We didn't know what else to do. She was married
and sent to live a town away.

"My father wouldn't allow me to visit her, but five
months later I got away on a clever excuse and paid her a
visit. I didn't care if my father would beat me for it later; I
had to see if she was all right.

"But she wasn't. When I saw her, she was with child, and
her face was as swollen as her belly. Her husband beat her.
She was certain he'd end up killing her just as she knew he
had his last two young wives.

"She tried to say goodbye, to tell me how much she loved
me, but I wouldn't let her. I promised her that I'd find a way
to save her, although I had no idea how. I was just a boy still,
even though the circumstances of my life led me to feel
much older—I was accustomed to handling responsibilities
much beyond those of my age. In our house, it was a matter
of survival.

"I asked Clarissa to hold on until I could come for her. She said she would, but her eyes told me that she didn't know if she'd be able. I raced home, crying all the way, allowing my horse to navigate. I was torn to pieces, and even after the three-hour journey home, I still had no idea how to help Clarissa.

"One day, I was in the servants' quarters when one of the servants ran into the kitchen, out of breath, her arms bundled with foods from the market. She'd heard a rumor in the market place.

"There was a magician traveling through Bundry. Well, not much of anyone traveled through Bundry. It wasn't the kind of place you came to unless you had a very good reason or you were stuck there. We thought that it might be a sign, and I resolved to go find him immediately.

"It took me the rest of the day to find him, but I did by nightfall. At first, the wizard wouldn't take me seriously. He kept dismissing me, saying I was just a young boy, to leave him alone. But after a lot of convincing and the little bit of wealth I could come up with, he agreed to help me. I wore him down."

A half-hearted smile formed across his face. "He told me that he'd never had anyone pestered him so much to get his way, and that if I was this stubborn about it, perhaps he should just go ahead and teach me. He said it took a lot of persistence to learn magic, and I'd already shown him that I had that.

"Despite his reluctant agreement to teach me, he said he couldn't intervene on behalf of Clarissa. All he could do was teach me to do so myself, he said."

I knew Marcelo's story didn't have a happy ending. This was not an exciting story about his beginnings in magic. It was the tragic story of his cruel beginnings, and he was right: They were similar to mine.

"I snuck out to see the magician as often as I could. He taught me and I proved to be an apt student, more gifted than most. The magician was pleased with me. But no matter how quickly I learned, it wasn't fast enough. We received news of Clarissa's 'accidental' death three months later."

I gasped even though I suspected this was how Marcelo's story would end.

"According to her husband, Clarissa fell down the stairs, clumsy with her big belly." Marcelo spit the words out.

My hand at my chest, I searched for something to say but found nothing.

"My mother mourned in her own quiet way. But not my father. According to him, it was a sad accident and just the way of life. He moved on, although I'd be shocked if some rumors of how Clarissa's husband treated her hadn't reached my father's ears. After all, he controlled the whole area."

"What did you do?" I asked. How could he recover from that kind of heartbreak?

"I ran away. I begged the magician to take me away from there, to take me with him. He was worried about taking Bundry's sole surviving heir. He knew that to be a serious offense, and he refused for so long that I thought I'd be stuck in Bundry forever.

"But he knew what my life was like at court there, and he

felt sorry for me. Finally, once I convinced him that I wouldn't change my mind, he agreed, as long as we hid my location. I haven't been back since."

"Marcelo, I'm so, so sorry." There were no words that could fix it.

I watched him brush the starts of a tear away and compose himself immediately. Had I not known, I wouldn't have been able to tell that he'd been upset at all. His steely resolve came from years of practice.

"Now do you understand why I can't take you back to Norland? It would be subjecting you to the same cruel fate as Clarissa. I was unable to help her then, but I can help you now. It won't make up for what happened, but it's the right thing to do."

I nodded. I still didn't want him to put so much at risk for me, but I did understand now. And secretly, in the part of me that was terrified of a life with Winston, I was grateful. I could use his help. I had no one else to turn to.

PLOTS, PLANS, AND A DESTINATION

"*Is* Albacus the magician who taught you?"

We were moving again. We'd switched horses to give the ones we'd ridden so hard from Lake Creston a break. The tired horses trailed behind us, their reins tied to our saddles.

"How could you possibly know that name?"

"He wrote you a dedication at the beginning of *The Magyke of the Elementes.*"

"I see." His response was terse. "Albacus did teach me magic, but he isn't the one who came to Bundry. It was Albacus' brother, Mordecai."

"Where did you go with Mordecai?"

"I stayed with him and Albacus at their estate to the east. It was just far enough away that my father wouldn't find me easily, though I'm sure he looked for me. I'm his only remaining heir, and he'd counted on me to take over Bundry. But Albacus put a spell over the estate so that he couldn't find me as long as I stayed there. And he never did."

"Are your father and mother still living?" I asked.

"I neither know nor care."

"Is that how you'll keep me away from my father too? By casting a spell so he can't find me?"

"I'd prefer to find another way that doesn't burn our bridges."

"Then where are we going now?"

Marcelo sped up his horse to come level with me. "How many questions can you ask? I don't know where we're going yet. None of this went the way I planned it. Now, can we enjoy some silence?" And with that he passed me. I was left to follow the horse that trailed behind his.

Marcelo was putting a physical buffer between us. I imagined that talking about personal issues made him uncomfortable. I saw him muttering to himself up ahead. It was probably best that I couldn't hear what he was saying.

Of course I had questions. I had myriad questions. I had no footing in this new life that was unfolding. I didn't know where we were going, what we'd do once we got there, or how Marcelo would keep me away from Father and Winston.

But I kept up with Marcelo. He was my only hope.

I allowed my thoughts to drift toward happier places. I wondered how Gertrude was. Was she enjoying the gardens and the lakes now that spring was almost here? Were the roses budding yet? I hoped Maggie would think to get a message to Gertrude explaining the truth of what happened. I didn't want Gertrude to worry.

I was safer in the company of a discontented, grumbling

magician that I barely knew than I was in my own home with my blood family. The world was a crazy place.

I held my head high and pointed my horse at an angle. I came up on Marcelo's left. If he didn't know where we were going or what we were doing, then I'd better work on the problem too. I didn't know what a girl like me could possibly contribute, but I decided that it wouldn't be from a lack of trying.

~

*M*arcelo secured lodging for us at an inn with stables. Stable hands would take care of our horses while we had a meal and rested. I couldn't decide what I needed more: food and water or a bed. Marcelo decided for me, guiding me into the tavern that was part of the inn.

He pulled my chair out for me. I winced as I sat.

"Are you hurt?" he asked.

I barely found the energy to shake my head. Since we'd stopped, the exhaustion from riding all day and the stress of the encounter with Winston settled within me as heavily as a rock.

"I'm not injured, but every part of my body does hurt. I'm not accustomed to riding as long as we did." I immediately tried to fix what I said. "I'm sure I'll feel fine after a night's rest." I didn't want to sound as if I were complaining. I was grateful for all he was doing for me.

"I was thinking, you should dispatch a missive to my father right away, before he sends someone to look for me.

You could say that Winston appeared with a band of his men at Lake Creston, threatening to take me by force, and I became most unsettled.

"You worried because of my fragile health. I'd only just started to show signs of possible recovery. You asked Winston to leave, and he refused, drawing his sword. You felt obligated to protect me, certain that's what the Count of Norland would want, and you rode away with me until you resolved the issue and ensured my safety.

"Maggie stayed behind because of the urgency of Winston's threat. Now, with my nerves in a terrible state due to Winston's harsh actions and words, I've fallen dangerously ill again. You've secured a room for me at an inn where you're caring for me, aiding in my recovery. You advise against the Count or the Countess coming to see me, as you fear my condition is still quite contagious.

"You seek that the Count advise you. What would he have you do? There's a safe location of some sort—this part I haven't figured out yet—that you could take me to, where I'd be safe and tended to until I can heal, if he gives his permission. You can secure a lady's maid for me there as soon as we arrive."

Marcelo's eyebrows rose in increments as I spoke. I thought his black eyebrows couldn't stretch any higher, until I spoke again.

"And you should ask him for funds to continue my care too."

The eyebrows gave one last fraction of an inch.

I shrugged. "We'll need to pay our way, and he'll expect to pay you if what you say is true."

169

"You worked this all out while we rode?"

I nodded.

He eyed me appraisingly. "Very well then. I'll do as you suggest. However, I won't leave you alone here to tend to the message. I'll do it after we eat and you're in your room."

I had never been in a tavern before. It wasn't the kind of place that the daughter of a Count frequented. It only took one quick look around to understand Marcelo's prudence. The clientele did not look trustworthy.

"And as far as where we'll go, I know now," Marcelo said. "While you were plotting out all of that, I was considering our alternatives. We'll go to Albacus and Mordecai and hope they receive us well."

"What do you mean 'hope they receive us well'?"

"You'll soon see. We're only a few days of riding from there."

Marcelo then turned to the innkeeper to place our order.

WHAT IS WITHIN BUBBLES FORTH

*W*hen Marcelo woke me early the next morning, my body clamored for more rest. But he pointed out that Winston was likely already searching for us and that we wouldn't be safe until we reached Albacus and Mordecai's stronghold. It was all the persuasion I needed to get out of bed right away.

We broke our fast with a quick bite of bread and cider and were back on the road. We alternated horses again, letting the ones we rode the day before trail behind us without the burden of a rider.

I feared what Father would do even now if he discovered that I was in good health. Were there still days left to meet the Count of Chester's deadline? I'd lost count in the confusion of the last several days. There might still be a day left. With great sadness, I knew that Father would still marry me away to Winston, even after his menacing behavior toward me.

I shook the thoughts away. They were making me

anxious. The sun was bright; it warmed my face above my coat collar pleasantly. I would let the sun melt thoughts of Father away. I forced a smile, hoping the real thing would come soon.

"How far do we have to go today?"

"We have to make it to Dunladun by tomorrow, thus we can stop somewhere around the halfway point when we're ready to rest for the night. Once we arrive in Dunladun, we'll wait there until we receive a response from the Count, your father. I told him to send reply to me there. If our strategy is to work, we need to make the Count believe that he's in control and that he wants you to stay away with me."

Marcelo was right. It was imperative that Father believe he was making the decisions, that he still dictated what happened in my life.

Now that I knew where we were going, my mind wandered. Marcelo led the way. All I had to do was follow.

I had never been very far from Norland, and I was surprised to notice that our surroundings, even after a full day of travel from Lake Creston, still looked very much like what I was accustomed to. The evergreen trees we passed were tall and full. The other trees were also old with thick trunks.

My thoughts meandered across topics of little relevance to the recent urgency that tinged my life, until it finally dawned on me. "Marcelo! Why don't you talk of magic while we travel? We have nothing better to do, and that way I can begin learning. You yourself have told me how much there is for me to learn and how long it'll take."

Marcelo sighed heavily, a bit unpleasantly even. "I

suppose you're right. The sooner you understand magic, the better for all of us."

He sighed yet again, in case I'd missed his reluctance the first time. "I've been thinking that perhaps I should teach you differently than Albacus and Mordecai taught me. Tell me exactly what happened when you were in the bathtub and the fire-water burned you."

I gave Marcelo a look.

"I know you think you've told me everything already, but let's explore it again. We may discover something new this time."

I swallowed my frustration at rehashing the old instead of learning the new and began. "I was taking a bath when I noticed the candle flames reflecting on the water. They were beautiful. I watched them for a while without doing anything or thinking about much of anything until my eyes lost focus, and—"

"I know what you did," Marcelo interrupted.

"I just told you, I didn't do anything at all."

"Oh, but you did. Subtle things perhaps, but in magic, the subtle is important. In fact, sometimes it's the most important factor of all."

"Then what did I do?"

"Well, you looked at the flames with unfocused eyes. You appreciated the beauty of fire and just let the fire be and do whatever it wanted to do."

"Yeah, burn me."

"Burning is fire's nature. Perhaps it was putting on a show to reward your appreciation."

"But how did it burn me when the flame wasn't even in

the water? The water burned me. Water should put out fire not burn."

"Yes, that's curious. Very curious. I haven't quite figured out that part of it yet. Now tell me of your experience with the fire in the hearth. Let's see what we can find in common between the occurrences."

"I was sitting, watching the fire. I thought it was beautiful. I watched the fire until my eyes lost focus, and I didn't think much of anything at all. The next thing I knew, you were yelling at me."

"Yes. The fire had almost encircled the room. Did you notice the things in common between both situations?"

"Yes," I said, reluctantly admitting that Marcelo was right in having us review the incidents again. "I watched the flames until my eyes lost focus, and I thought the fire was beautiful but didn't think of anything else."

"That's right," Marcelo said. "That's important to know. It seems you're doing magic by not trying to do it at all. That's most interesting indeed."

"Others do magic like that too, right?"

"Not that I've heard of. Perhaps Albacus and Mordecai won't be cross with me for bringing you to them after all. They'll find you most interesting."

"Will they not want me there?"

Marcelo turned to me, for once with a look of sympathy. "They're not always the friendliest sort, but that's only until you get to know them. Everything will be fine," and, after a pause, "I hope."

"You hope?"

"You told me that you were able to do one of the experiments with water from *The Magyke of the Elementes*, but we didn't have the chance to discuss it. Tell me about it now."

This time, I didn't mind recounting my experience. Talking distracted me from aching thighs and buttocks.

"Maggie had set a glass pitcher with water on the bedside table. While lying in bed, I looked at the water until my eyes lost focus and I forgot what I was trying to do. And that's when the water sloshed, I guess."

"Aha!" Marcelo sounded triumphant. "And did you feel appreciation for the water also? Did you think of its beauty?"

"I'm not sure if I did or not. I can't remember."

"But again you looked at the element until you weren't thinking about anything anymore, until you barely saw it. This is very important to know. This worked for you with fire and water."

"I suppose so."

"Oh, but wait. That may not be entirely true."

"What do you mean?"

"When you were relaxing by the lake the other day, you made the water bubble, and you were laying back against the blanket with your eyes closed when it happened."

"You were watching me?" I was shocked that he spied on me when I thought I was alone.

"Of course I watch you. You're not only my student but also my charge. I'm responsible for you, and inexplicable things keep happening to you. The sooner I'm able to understand what's going on, the sooner I can teach you how to protect yourself.

"Besides, if I hadn't been watching you, I wouldn't know

that you made the water of the lake bubble. Did you know that you did?"

I'd started to think, *Wow, he's snooty*, when I registered what he actually said.

I didn't answer his question. I couldn't have done something like that without even knowing it, could I?

"The surface of the water bubbled. Big, wide bubbles covered the water of Lake Creston as far as I could see, although they seemed to concentrate close to you. They held though you never looked at them. Then, from where I stood in the house, it appeared that you fell asleep. After you did, the bubbles gradually began to pop. And that was it."

I was quiet for a good while. It was challenging enough for me to accept that I was causing unusual and dangerous reactions with the elements when I was somewhat aware of it. Now to consider that I might be doing things like this when I didn't even know it made me extremely uncomfortable. How would I know what I could do and whom I might hurt in the process?

"Are you certain it was I who caused the lake to bubble like you say?" My hopeful question was hard to hear over the plodding of our four horses.

Marcelo's response was prompt and strong. "Without a doubt, it was you, and this forces us to modify our hypothesis of how you're doing this magic. We can no longer say that you create the magic through your sight, because that wasn't the case with the lake.

"How do you do it? How did you cause most of Lake Creston's water to form into bubbles without even willing it? How's that even possible? It makes no sense. It shouldn't be possible."

I didn't answer his questions. I knew even less about all of this than he did. Even so, I was the one causing these mysterious events.

"Do you remember anything helpful about your time by the lake, laying on the blanket? Were you perhaps thinking of bubbling water?"

I shook my head.

"Think, Clara. Is there anything that you were thinking or doing that could have done this?"

I shook my head again. This time, I blinked back tears. I didn't want Marcelo to see how this was affecting me.

"Come on, Clara, there must be something you can tell me that would help us figure this out."

I was silent again. I didn't understand why I was feeling so emotional.

Marcelo misinterpreted my silence as apathy.

"Clara!"

"Yes! I hear you. What do you want me to say? That I have no idea what in the world is going on? That I have absolutely no notion of how I could have caused a lake to bubble? I wasn't thinking about anything when I lay on the blanket. I was just relaxing. These last two months have been very difficult for me.

"I suffered from delusional fever for most of a month. Then I burned my entire body from the neck down, without even knowing how I did it. Every inch of my body stung and hurt terribly until I finally *un*burned my body, again without knowing how.

"My parents are cruel, desiring to give me away to an even crueler boy of a man, who will undoubtedly torture me in one way or another for the rest of my life. Blessedly, I'll probably die young from heartbreak and abuse, after bearing multiple children to continue the horrible chain of suffering.

"I had to leave the only home I've ever known and my beloved sister, Gertrude, the only person who's ever understood me. Now I've had to leave even Maggie behind. And who do I have to accompany me? You, and you don't even like me or care to have me around. You're waiting for the opportunity to be rid of me. Perhaps you'll have the chance once we reach Albacus and Mordecai's, even though you tell me it's likely that they'll be reluctant to have me there.

"Oh, and furthermore, my life and everything I've ever understood of it is turned upside down. It appears that I can do magic, even though I know absolutely nothing about magic. But that doesn't seem to interfere with my ability to keep hurting myself in agonizing ways. And did I mention it? If anyone were to find out that I can do magic, they'd likely burn me at the stake or submit me to some other hideous form of torture. Even Father might not be able to protect me from the townspeople if they suspect I'm some kind of witch."

Marcelo didn't say a word. He just looked at me, and that made it worse. I fought the tears back with difficulty. They burned hot in my eyes, and I was certain my face was red.

"I'm sixteen. This is a lot for me. So excuse me if it overwhelms me when you surprise me by saying that, not only am I doing dangerous magic that I don't understand when I'm somewhat aware of it, but that I'm also doing it when I don't even know it. It's a lot for me to handle, and you have no solutions for me. You don't understand me. *I* don't understand me."

I couldn't hold the tears back any longer, and I was starting to feel embarrassed by my outburst. Without another word, I motioned my horse to speed up. I trotted past Marcelo, so that the horse without rider that trailed behind connected by a rope lined up with him.

I didn't turn to look. I knew Marcelo might think me an immature girl, but I needed to say what I had. Everyone, including Marcelo, had rushed me from one place or thing to the next, without a thought of how it was affecting me.

Father and Mother treated me like a pawn in their strategy that prioritized wealth and prestige. The Count and Countess of Chester had treated me the same, with their son, Winston, acting as if I were his plaything, with which he had the right to do as he pleased. Only Samuel had been a touch of kindness in the midst of parental plotting, but it was unlikely that I would ever see him again.

In his stormy way, Marcelo made it clear that I was simply an obligation or a burden, depending on his mood. He looked for the way to fulfill his responsibility toward me so as to be free of it.

I missed Gertrude's affection and loving support so terribly just then that it physically hurt. When would I see her again? I cared very much that Marcelo would see me crying, but I couldn't hold the sadness back any longer. I cried with feminine composure and restraint as much as possible, but I cried.

I cried for a long time, my dependable horse leading the way to Dunladun, even though I had no idea where Dunladun was. And when no tears were left to shed, I discovered acceptance for my position in life. I rode in comforting silence for a long time, until Marcelo called from behind that it was time to stop for food and drink.

~

We stopped for the night at the halfway point to Dunladun. We had another long trek ahead of us the next day, but at least now we would rest. I walked into the inn gingerly, as exhausted from riding as I was from emotional release.

Marcelo found us a remote table to dine at, apart from the regular rowdy customers. Sparse conversation punctuated our dinner. I said almost nothing and was relieved when Marcelo deposited me in my room and left me. In minutes, I had washed up and was in bed.

Sleep was merciful. It came swiftly, and it took every unpleasantness with it. I slept soundly until the sun peeked through curtain-less windows.

OUTRUNNING THAT WHICH CANNOT BE OUTRUN

We rode side by side, every step taking us closer to Dunladun. I woke with a fresh outlook. I resolved to accept how things were and to learn all that I could about magic. If this was where my life was leading, then it was important that I understand my gifts. Perhaps I could find power in a life that had been devoid of it.

Marcelo treated me with unusual compassion and consideration, as if my outburst had led him to see what he hadn't before. He'd started treating me as a young girl, one that he needed to make allowances for. That's not what I wanted, but I had no desire to say anything about it then. He would soon witness my transformation.

The day was quiet, with both of us immersed in our own thoughts. The rhythmic melody of horse steps was mesmerizing, and it lulled me into a peaceful calm.

What happened next occurred without my conscious

decision, just as when I'd accidentally made the lake bubble, except that later on I would remember it all, as if I'd been a casual and unconcerned observer watching myself from outside my body.

It began with a rumbling of the earth so tenuous that it was difficult to differentiate between it and the pounding of hooves.

Then there was another rumble, still subtle, but more difficult to dismiss. I, however, continued to stare ahead, oblivious.

Marcelo turned my way. If he'd been an animal, his ears would have pricked in alertness and his tail stood on end as he anticipated *something*.

Marcelo might have attempted to interfere with what I was inadvertently doing then. But he didn't. He'd been absent when I'd affected fire, and he'd been a remote witness when I caused the lake to bubble. Observing me through the process up close could provide the understanding to help me control my powers.

A third rumble shook the earth and commanded attention. The ground moved for only moments, but it was more than sufficient to panic the horses.

They tried to shake free of their riders.

Instincts from years of riding kicked in. I squeezed the reins tightly with one hand, wrapped my other arm around my horse's neck, and clamped my thighs around his body while I leaned in to him. Had I been riding sidesaddle, I would have fallen.

Once the horse returned his fore legs to the ground, I secured my other arm around his neck too. When he jumped again, I was nestled into him as closely as I could be. My face pressed against his neck, and I remained peaceful. My body was there, but I was someplace else.

My serenity affected my horse. He was the first to settle.

The other horses continued with their resistance. Those that trailed behind us, attached only by ropes, jumped and pulled at their fastenings. Their instincts screamed at them to run away, though they had nowhere to run to. The earth that shook surrounded them, corralling them.

Marcelo had anticipated what might come, and he was prepared for his horse to rear, already soothing the animal.

But then it happened again. This time it was worse. There was no calming the horses anymore.

The earth rose beneath us in undulating ripples. As if the earth magic radiated out from beneath me, it continued in waves, up and out in every direction. The road that had looked solid moments before was malleable, and I was shaking it out like one would a dusty rug, over and again.

The horses were uncontrollable. They fought for their survival. As they couldn't free themselves of us, they took us with them. They raced ahead on the road, as if they could beat the rolling motion with speed and determination. They tried to outrun the magic with everything they had.

But they couldn't. Not so long as I was astride my horse. And I was. I held onto my horse as if my life depended upon it, which it did—had I fallen, the horse that galloped behind me would have trampled me.

My horse and I moved as one seamless creature, and we took the earthquake with us as we went. It was localized, and I was its centralized focal point.

By this time, Marcelo was attempting to stop me. However, I was impervious to his shouts. The horses were loud, my stupor profound, and Marcelo seemed a world away.

The dirt road continued to roll beneath us, giving the surreal impression that the horses were riding the crest of a continuous wave, trying desperately to stay on it to avoid the crashing surf.

The horses charged. Their muscles, streamlined for just this kind of movement, performed at peak efficiency. We sped toward Dunladun, our very lives the motivation.

I remained entranced, bewitched by my own wandering mind, and noticed nothing.

Eventually, after longer than I could have ever imagined possible, I snapped out of it.

It wasn't because of anything Marcelo did or said, nor was it because of the horses' desperate fleeing. The moment was simply complete and over.

I came to, and as soon as I did, the earth stilled.

Nonetheless, the horses continued to run.

Too agitated to notice that their surroundings had settled, it took Marcelo several minutes of determined reassurance to get the lead horses to reduce their speed to a trot.

Once the horses realized the earth was unmoving, they ground to a halt. Their breathing came heavy and loud. Sweat coated their bodies. Muscles twitched and bulged.

I found Marcelo. He stared right back at me, eyes, a startling blue, wide and intense. He glowered until I wanted to turn away.

He swiveled in his saddle, taking in our surroundings. A small town was visible atop the crest of the upcoming hill.

"We'll stop there," he said. "The horses need water and rest. And we need to talk."

Marcelo didn't wait for my response. He was in control again.

At first, the horses resisted Marcelo's signals to move. But his voice was stern, and the horses and I obeyed.

We made our way to the town slowly. The horses were tired. The monotonous sound of hooves hitting earth reigned again, but this time I was careful not to let myself become distracted by it. Although the dreaminess lingered, I was beginning to understand that I might have caused the uproar.

When we finally arrived at the town, we found that it was smaller than it had appeared, and we were lucky to find a countrywoman with a modest cottage willing to take us in and feed us in exchange for a few coins.

Her teenage son tended to the horses. We could see them through her kitchen window. They drank greedily and ate some grass, but then they sank to the ground in uncommon horse behavior.

The woman noticed it too. "Ya been running those horses hard, eh?" I had to interpret dropped consonants and clipped vowels.

Marcelo tried to brush her comment away. "Yes, we're on our way to Dunladun. We must arrive there by nightfall."

"Well ya should have no problem doing that. Yer only a few hours away. But ya must let them horses rest first."

The woman turned her attention back to the stew and

bread she was sharing with us, and Marcelo gave me a sharp look. I couldn't tell if he was angry with me, at himself, or both.

"Well, at least we made good time," he said. "We'll talk after we eat."

Obviously we wouldn't talk about what happened in front of our curious hostess. I nodded meekly, not sure how I felt about our impending talk. Part of me dreaded the upcoming discussion, another looked forward to it. I was ready to understand what was happening to me and to take control—at least I thought I was.

The matron excused herself, saying she had washing to tend to, and left us alone. Still, Marcelo let it go while we ate. The woman's stew, though meager in its ingredients, was very tasty, the result of a cook skilled with spices and making do. Marcelo and I ate hungrily, sopping up the last bits of stew with bread baked that morning, but we didn't ask for seconds.

With the taste of ale still on our lips, we found a spot under a tree that the sun warmed. My tailbone screamed at me as I sat, but we settled in. We could see the horses from there. As soon as they started moving again, we would continue on our journey.

I leaned my back into the tree trunk and sighed loudly. Finally, I turned toward Marcelo.

"Y ou had no idea that you were causing the earth to shake, did you?"

So it had been me.

Marcelo's voice sounded surprisingly calm. "I watched you very closely this time, and it didn't look like you were aware of what you were doing in the least."

"I wasn't." This fact was both terrifying and thrilling— terrifying because I still had no control over something so dangerous and powerful, and thrilling because I could only begin to imagine what I would be capable of doing once I understood it better.

"Again, you were thinking of nothing at all when it happened, is that right?"

I nodded. Marcelo was looking straight at me. "That's what I thought."

"So what do we do now?"

"You must learn to control what you're doing. You go someplace else when you connect to the elements. Once I tried to stop you, I yelled at you and you didn't hear me."

"You yelled at me?" I was shocked that I wouldn't hear him; he'd ridden right next to me.

"Yes, I yelled at you repeatedly, but it didn't matter how loud I got or what I said, you remained wherever you were. You didn't even notice that your horse was rearing, trying to throw you."

I didn't know whether to be alarmed or amazed. "My horse reared?"

"Several times. I was grateful that you have obviously

been taught to ride well. You held on tightly and leaned into your horse. But it didn't distract you from where you were."

"I didn't know." My voice was softer this time as I turned to look at my horse. Aware now of his revolt, I looked at him differently, with distrust, though I didn't suppose it was fair to blame him for what he'd done.

"It's truly incredible that you didn't realize what was happening. Your horse was jumping, I was yelling at you, and the earth was shaking beneath you. And still, you were able to remain so intrinsically connected to the earth element. You have a connection with the elements I've never seen or heard of before."

I turned toward Marcelo again. I had an idea of what that might mean even before he said it, and I felt a surge of excitement for the first time, despite the gravity of the situation.

"That means you may have some of the most powerful magic in existence brewing within you, just waiting for you to connect with it and learn to use it."

Marcelo studied me with dark, hooded eyes, and I wished desperately to know what he was thinking. Whether he liked it or not, he'd become a part of whatever was happening to me.

"What happens next, Marcelo?" I asked. After a lifetime of my parents planning out every one of my steps, where I could anticipate the details of my future all too clearly, I had no real idea what to expect.

"We ride to Dunladun and wait there for your father's message. As soon as it arrives, we ride again. It's even more urgent than I'd previously realized that I get you to Albacus and Mordecai. They have much more experience than I do. They may have seen this before."

I chuckled without meaning to, and Marcelo's head whipped my way accusingly. He had just lived through a harrowing experience because of me, and now I was laughing?

"You don't have to look at me like that. I understand how serious this all is. It's just that I've always felt forgettable in my life in Norland. My parents barely pay attention to me, unless it's to marry me away, and no one other than Gertrude cared much about what I did. I was never particularly good at anything, nor was I particularly bad at anything. I led an average, forgettable life.

"Then suddenly I become this anomaly with skills you've never seen before and that I don't even know how to control. It's a bit funny how life takes these unexpected turns, and we have no way of knowing when they're coming. Don't you think so?"

No, Marcelo didn't think so. He glowered at me, which made me chortle again.

"Sorry, I can't help myself. Maybe I'm just delirious from the intensity of the last many weeks."

I looked away from the angry magician to compose myself, and when my face was sufficiently serious for his liking, I turned back to face him. "It looks like it might still be awhile before the horses are ready."

The horses hadn't moved since they lay down, fatigue and the aftermath of adrenaline keeping them put.

"Do you think maybe I should practice a little magic

with you while we wait? Try to make some progress with learning to control it?"

"No! I've had quite enough of your magic for one day. The horses have rested enough. We ride to Dunladun now. And for the love of everything holy, try to keep your mind from wandering. Don't even *think* about the air." And he stalked off, toward the horses.

I watched him for a second, frustrated. Then I stood and tried to brush the dust from my dress. But there was no point. After days of riding without a change of clothing, my dress was dirty, brown around the hem. Mother would be horrified to see me like this.

There was nothing I could do about it. I had neither coins nor influence. I was on the run. I just wasn't sure what I was running from anymore.

Were we still running from Winston, or were we running from me now?

BEAUTY WITHIN MAGIC

*D*unladun was far larger than I anticipated. I'd heard of the town to the northeast of Norland before (visitors shared stories of their travels with Father and Mother) but I never realized how densely populated it was. People rushed here and there, sometimes with baskets or bundles under their arms, sometimes on their way to pick them up. Children played in the streets, their loud calls barely audible over the clacking of horse hooves and the general bustling of the town.

The streets were dirty, with refuse visible everywhere. Even so, my disheveled state made me uncomfortable. Upon our horses, we passed ladies in high fashion, with colorful dresses, elaborate collars, and feathered hats. My dress had once been as fine as any I saw, but not anymore. Several women cast haughty looks my way.

Marcelo seemed to know where he was going. We made our way down the middle of the main street, passing other riders along the way. Pedestrians kept to the sidewalks to

LUCÍA ASHTA

avoid piles of manure, only jetting across the street when they needed to.

We rode past varied storefronts, and I wished I had the luxury to explore the town. It was far more exciting than Norland. There were markets and tradesmen as in Norland, but there were also merchants of fine goods. I longed to see the fine papers, inks, and stamps, and to purchase a leather-bound sketchbook for my new adventures. We passed a bookstore, and the urge to peruse its inventory was so strong that my horse felt it and momentarily slowed.

But Marcelo kept his gaze forward and our path straight. He didn't startle and turn to look as I did when two boys shouted at each other from opposite sides of the street, nor did he jump when a man whistled loudly at a passerby that hadn't seen him.

My horse walked next to Marcelo's obediently; there was nothing I needed to do. My head swiveled left and right. By the time we reached the inn, I was nearly dizzy from the overwhelming sights and sounds, and it was a great relief to finally dismount and head inside.

However, the interior was dim and cold in comparison to the sunshiny, colorful outdoors, and I thought the over-stimulation was better than this. In the end, my preference didn't matter. Marcelo told me to sit in a chair removed from the comings and goings of the inn staff and their patrons while he arranged our lodging, and I did.

Once I sat, my body sped toward exhaustion. I didn't want to get back up, not even to go outside and take in more of the sights of city life. The recent days had been long and arduous.

By the time Marcelo returned to fetch me, I'd melted like butter into the chair. I felt him standing over me, and I opened my eyes.

"I thought you were asleep. Do you want to eat or would you rather skip dinner and go to your room to sleep?"

I thought about it for a moment. Sleep sounded divine. Yet my stomach spoke up with a noticeable rumble and made the decision for me.

Marcelo looked me up and down like he hadn't in a while. "You should probably head upstairs to clean up first."

"I can't do much about my appearance. I really wish I could. I'm very uncomfortable like this. But I have no change of clothing, and my dress is filthy from the dust of travel and the sweat of horses. I don't even have a comb to run through my hair."

I tried to run my fingers through my tangled curls and grimaced. My hair had never been in this state before. I would have quite the time getting it back to normal.

From the look on Marcelo's face, it was clear he hadn't thought of any of this.

"Perhaps once Father's delivery arrives, we can purchase a new dress for me," I said.

Marcelo was shaking his head even before I'd finished. "We won't have time to visit a seamstress. I'm hoping that the Count's message will arrive by morning, and we can depart immediately after. You'll have to wait until we make it to Albacus and Mordecai's estate to have dresses made for you."

"I can understand that. But, Marcelo, I can't look like

this, if for nothing else than the fact that it will draw attention to us. I need clothes that at least *look* clean."

Marcelo studied me some more. "Yes, I suppose you're right. Your appearance does raise questions. You're clearly from a noble line, yet your clothing no longer matches that noblesse. I think I may be able to do something to hold you over until we reach our destination. Follow me to our rooms so we can have some privacy."

As I followed Marcelo up creaky stairs, I wondered what he could do to repair my disheveled appearance. Even if I attempted to wash my dress, there wouldn't be enough time for it to dry if we were to leave by morning.

Marcelo ushered me into my room. It was small and quaint, but the bed looked very inviting. I looked at it longingly.

I heard the click of the door locking, and I turned. I stood without moving, very aware of my steady breath as I watched him and waited.

He met my eyes only briefly, but his stare was intense when he did. I couldn't tell what erupted in his gaze, but something did. I was sure of it.

He took two steps toward me and stopped. "Close your eyes."

Instinctively, I took a small step away from him, farther toward the window. "Why do I need to close my eyes?"

Marcelo huffed. "Just close your eyes, Clara. I can't do this with you watching me."

I deliberated for longer than I probably should have but, finally, I closed my eyes.

Marcelo started right away. I couldn't tell what exactly

he was doing, but I knew he was doing something. The air around me had turned electric, and my skin tingled.

It continued for several minutes before I couldn't resist any longer. I disobeyed his wishes, and I peeked my eyes open.

Luckily, his were closed. I forcibly suppressed my reaction so he wouldn't notice I was now watching him. He was doing wonderful magic! Dirt specks floated in the air around me, and Marcelo continued to pull more from my dress. Already, the yellow fabric looked brighter.

Even though it was dirt that hung suspended in the air, it was beautiful. Sunlight streamed in through the window behind me to skip across the dirt motes, lighting them up. I felt as if I were within a snow globe. I only had one back at home in Norland, but it was one of my few treasures. It whisked me away to the places of dreams in an instant.

The dirt swirled around me in that same way, and concerns instantly melted away—they couldn't exist within a charmed snow globe! I smiled. I lit up too, and it wasn't because of the sunshine that set my hair ablaze.

I shifted my gaze back to Marcelo. For the first time, I noticed how beautiful he was. Maybe it was the magic, or maybe it was the snow globe effect. Whatever it was, he looked magnificent.

Dark, thick lashes spread against his cheeks, contrasting with a tanned complexion. Unruly hair tumbled across his forehead, softening the angular features of his face. A straight nose punctuated the curve in his upper lip.

Marcelo stood strong, with hands slightly out to the side, pointing toward me. He appeared unaware that I studied him. His dark coat hung open, and his clothes clung to him in enough places to show that the body beneath was muscular. It made me wonder what Marcelo had done with his life before I met him. I still knew only scant highlights of his history, and even then, only the tragic ones.

More grime floated and surrounded me, and I couldn't help but feel contented with the pleasantness of the scene. Then Marcelo began to bring the dirt together, coalescing it into one form. Dirt specks hovered in the air, moving where he wanted them, until they merged.

I realized he might soon be finished, and I quickly closed my eyes, hoping that my venture into Marcelo's private world of magic would remain secret.

But he took a few minutes longer. I squirmed, wondering if I would soon be able to open my eyes.

He cleared his throat. "You can open your eyes now, Clara."

When I did, he wouldn't meet them. He looked away, pretending to be distracted by the features of the bedroom. The room contained only a simple bed, a small table with a candelabrum and basin, and a plain chair. It was then that I realized he'd studied me just as I'd studied him.

I was surprised that it made him uncomfortable. He'd examined me many times before, with my eyes open.

I turned toward the window before I allowed my smile to come forth. My life had become much more interesting since Marcelo entered it.

~

*D*inner was simple yet entirely satisfactory after our long journey. I could barely think of anything except sleep, but Marcelo had arranged a bath for me, and I was infinitely grateful for the hot water.

I lingered in the metal tub contentedly, blocked off from two other patrons by wooden screens. None of us said a word, and I was grateful for the silence and semblance of privacy. The innkeeper who led me into the bath said I could stay as long as I wanted, but I was afraid if I stayed too long, I would fall asleep. Already, my eyes were droopy.

In the water, I discovered that every part of me ached. The water brought my body's soreness to the surface only to immediately work on pacifying it. I couldn't remember the last time I was this comfortable.

That's when I recalled my last bath experience. I was immersed in a tub much like this when the water burned me. I started to panic and immediately tried to put a stop to it. But it was difficult. I had this strong effect over the elements, and I didn't know how to prevent injuring myself because of it.

My eyes flared wide as I struggled to prevail over my worry. I forced myself to look away from the candles in the room and to keep my mind from becoming distracted with abstract thoughts about the water. I might not have much control yet, but I could prevent replicating the exact conditions from my last bath.

My bathing experience wasn't all that relaxing anymore. I sighed. I had to figure this out soon.

I could just get it over with, clean up quickly and head

back to my room. However, the stubborn streak in me refused. I deserved this time to myself for relaxation. I would do my best to keep from thinking of any element, but after that, it just would have to be whatever it was.

Until I learned to control my powers, I would do my best not to let them control me. I let my eyelids close all the way.

I lost track of time, only leaving the water once it had grown tepid. I walked on rubbery legs back to my room and opened the door straight into Marcelo.

～

"What are you doing here?" I asked.

"I went out while you bathed and bought you a comb. As you said, you need one."

"Oh, thank you!" I cleaned my hair in the bath, but I still couldn't run my fingers through it. "I really appreciate it, Marcelo."

He nodded. "I left it on the table, and I also filled your pitcher so you'll have water for the morning."

"Thank you." My gratitude was heartfelt. So far away from the comforts of home, these little gestures made a big difference.

"Is there anything else you need?"

"I don't think so. I can make do with what I have until we reach your teachers' estate."

"Get some rest. If we receive your father's message early tomorrow as I hope, we'll leave right away."

"Very well. Good night, Marcelo," I said as I closed and bolted the door behind him.

I walked straight to the table to find the comb. It was exquisite, silver decorated with mother of pearl, which must have cost Marcelo far more than our food and lodging. I skimmed my fingers across it.

Still, my tangled hair would have to wait until morning. Like a petulant child, exhaustion wouldn't allow me to deny it restorative sleep any longer.

My stiff dress clung to my moist skin uncomfortably. In moments, I had stripped myself of it. My muscles were loose from the hot water and happy to be free of constraint.

Fatigue took over my mind, and my feet walked me over to the bed. I'd never before slept naked, but I would that night. My undergarments were soiled from travel. I pulled back the covers, slid into the bed, and allowed sleep to have its way with me.

COMING AND GOING

I didn't wake early the next morning as I usually did. The sun had fully risen when I heard knocking at the door.

My dream was vivid, and its semblance of reality gripped me. I clutched the covers and turned onto my side. My clever dream incorporated the knocking seamlessly, as if it had planned it all along. The bed was warm from my captured body heat, and its comfort nudged me back into a deep sleep.

But the knocking wouldn't cease. After a few more times, my dream couldn't accommodate the sound any longer, and the knocking lured me awake. The realization that I had to answer the door weaved its way through a foggy mind, and I stumbled out of bed and bumped into the table.

With a fascinating lack of grace, I made my way to the door. With my hand reaching for the handle, the knock came again. I couldn't yet speak to tell the person on the other side that I was at the door. I turned the handle and pulled.

The door was locked.

I turned the bolt and pulled the door toward me again. I leaned into the open door, resting my head against its side. Through half open eyes, I found Marcelo on the other side of the threshold.

"Clara," he said, barely above a whisper, "it's time to wake."

"Mmmm," I mumbled while I stepped aside for him to come in.

Yet Marcelo didn't come in.

He didn't do or say anything at first.

He looked at me until his chest rose in a soft sigh.

Again speaking quietly, he said, "I'll wait out here while you dress."

I looked down at myself to discover waves of exposed flesh.

I looked back at him.

And then I shut the door on him without saying a single word.

&

It took more time to compose myself from the shock of opening the door to Marcelo while I was fully naked than it did to get dressed, even with all the elaborate steps that it entailed. After I pulled on undergarments, tunic, hose, dress, and collar, and struggled to tighten my bodice on my own, I was still embarrassed to see

Marcelo. But I assumed he was waiting for me on the other side of the door, and I couldn't just leave him there.

With a reminder that this man had already seen me naked when I was ill, I took in a deep, rallying breath, and opened the door again. Marcelo was there, leaning against the opposite wall with arms crossed, with a look that expressed the unlikely complements of amusement and impatience.

Without saying anything, I stepped aside, my arm gesturing inward. I had yet to comb my hair, but I couldn't leave Marcelo out there any longer. I blushed with the memory of my nudity as Marcelo slipped by me.

"Your father's messenger arrived in the night."

I was immediately grateful that he continued on with our morning as if nothing unusual had occurred.

"It seems that you do know how your father thinks. He did as you predicted he would. For the time being, he wants me to take you somewhere safe so you can heal and recover from the shock of the confrontation with Winston. He understands that you'll recover more rapidly if you feel secure and your nerves have the opportunity to settle. Interestingly, his missive said nothing about Winston's behavior or the fact that he showed up to take you with a troop of armed men."

This wasn't surprising. I recognized Father's priorities.

"As you predicted, he sent gold to compensate my efforts and to pay for your immediate needs. We can order you new dresses when we arrive at Albacus and Mordecai's."

I only nodded. A range of unexpected emotion was flurrying through me: familiar sadness and disappointment that my parents cared about me only because of what I could bring them, pangs of longing for Gertrude and her unconditional love for me, apprehension at what it would be like to meet Albacus and Mordecai, and intrigue and excitement at the prospect of learning about magic with Marcelo.

Some of this must have been apparent on my face, as Marcelo continued very gently. "It would be good for us to leave Dunladun right away. Will you be ready soon?"

"Yes, I'd just like to comb my hair first please."

"Of course. I'm all set. Is it all right if I wait here with you?"

I smiled shyly. "Yes, it is. Take a seat," I said while pointing to the lone chair. I picked up the comb and sat on the bed. There was no looking glass in the room, so it didn't matter where I sat.

I began the arduous work of untangling knots that had begun to mat. It took quite some time, but finally, I was able to brush the comb from my roots all the way down to the ends at my waist. Then I braided my hair quickly, twisted it up, and secured it the best I could with the comb. My hairdo didn't possess the elegance of Maggie's fine skill, but I hoped it would keep it from tangling all over again on the day's ride.

Relieved to be finished with the task, I looked over at Marcelo and discovered him following my every move.

"You remind me of Clarissa," he said, as if that explained it all—and I suppose that it did. I understood the love and longing for a sister.

"You look nothing like her; she was dark complexioned like me. But your ways remind me of her. I watched her comb her hair many times. She had long, curly hair like yours, though it was black of course. She moved like you when she combed her hair, as if she were in a dream and someplace else all together."

"I'm sorry you lost her. You must miss her very much."

"I do."

And then the moment was over.

"We're getting a later start than I wanted, but I think it would still be wise to break our fast here before beginning our trek. Are you ready to eat?"

"Yes, food sounds good."

Even as I answered he was looking around the room to see if I was leaving anything behind, but I had nothing extraneous to leave. Quickly, I poured water from the pitcher into the basin and splashed my face with it. And while I patted my face dry with a linen, he grabbed my coat for me. When I joined him, he ushered me out the door and down the stairs.

A few treads down, I discovered I had to say something. "You know, I don't usually sleep naked."

"You don't need to explain yourself, Clara."

Yet I felt that I did.

"I'd actually never slept naked before, but my under clothes didn't feel fresh after my bath. That's why I forgot that I was naked when I opened the door to you. I was half asleep."

I blushed at the memory as I continued down the stairs.

"It's all right, Clara, really. I didn't mind at all. Your body is beautiful."

I was grateful then that Marcelo was behind me and couldn't see my face. I flushed even more.

By the time we reached the ground floor, I was already working hard to push our conversation out of my mind. When Marcelo ordered our breakfast and turned his attention to the day of travel ahead, I was deeply relieved and, like him, I turned my thoughts away from the past to what we would find ahead.

$\sim$

*B*y the time we left Dunladun, the entire town was awake. I was again struck by how loud the city was when we exited the inn onto the street, where an attendant waited for us with our horses.

The clopping of horses and the cries of adults and children surrounded us. Like the previous day when we first arrived, I couldn't seem to focus on any one place.

"Will that be all, Mister?" the boy asked Marcelo.

"Yes, that'll be all."

The boy waited for Marcelo to tip him and then ran off.

Marcelo approached to help me mount my horse. I accepted his help even though I again rode in the saddle like a man. I already knew how weary the journey would be. I fully intended to make it as easy for myself as possible.

I looked at my yellow dress. Marcelo's magic made it look less dingy than it had been since we left Lake Creston. I lamented that the day's travels would probably leave it in no better shape than it had been the previous night.

"Do you think we might be able to purchase a hat for me

before we leave Dunladun? It would be nice to have something to shield me from the beating sun all day."

Marcelo looked hesitant.

"It needn't be an expensive one."

"It's not that. Your father sent sufficient funds to meet your needs." He looked toward the sun. It was still relatively low in the sky. "I suppose we can make time for a quick stop."

He tied one of the runaway horses to mine and one to his. Then we set off. I'd intended to ask Marcelo all about where we were going and how far away it was when two men burst out of a tavern a block up the street. Immediately, it became obvious they'd been up drinking all night. They fell into each other, trying to punch and hold all at once. Within seconds, half the tavern tumbled outside to watch the fight.

Marcelo didn't seem surprised by the drunkards that poured out of the tavern at early morning, but I'd never seen anything like it before, let alone right after breakfast.

He nudged the horses forward despite the conflict. He didn't slow our pace when we drew near but continued looking forward.

I couldn't help myself.

The fight was as ungainly as it was disturbing. Slovenly men lashed out at each other with drunken clumsiness, and those who watched screamed at them with blood thirst.

One of the onlookers caught me watching as we passed. He gave me a hateful look and spit on the ground while holding my gaze.

Mesmerized by the disgust I found in the man's eyes, my

own paused on him, but once I snapped them away, I didn't look back. Like Marcelo, I held my head high and my line of sight ahead. I tried to ignore the shiver that ran through my body; I knew the man stared at my back as we rode away.

I was tempted to ponder what I'd just witnessed, but there were too many distractions. Doors slammed shut, horses neighed, hammers and mallets clanged, church bells rang, children ran by us, and neighbors called to each other across the street. The cacophony prevented any thought.

And then there were the smells: bread baking, animals, and human waste. It was an unpleasant mélange. The bakeries lured my nose toward thoughts of pleasantness, only for the other more pungent odors to overwhelm them.

By the time we reached the midway point out of Dunladun, my senses were swirling uncomfortably, and I was anxious to leave. The shops I'd admired as we entered the town no longer held any appeal.

"Marcelo, I can get a hat later. Let's just leave. I'm finding the city unpleasant."

"Excellent. I've never much liked the place. I can't understand why so many people travel to visit it."

He navigated the horses around a cart in the middle of the street and then pointed them toward the town's exit.

Even the horses seemed to want to leave the din behind, and before long, we were free of it.

A WOMAN IN A MAN'S WORLD

*D*unladun gave me a new appreciation for the quiet of the open road. I didn't feel like talking for a long time, which seemed to suit Marcelo just fine.

We continued northeast. The woods surrounding us became denser. Less homesteads dotted the forest the farther from Dunladun we got. It was a pleasant view, despite its monotony.

"Marcelo, where exactly are we going? You never told me where Albacus and Mordecai live."

"They live in Irele."

"I've not heard of Irele before."

"You'll understand why once we get there," he said.

That didn't sound positive. "How far away is it?"

"From here it's about a three-day ride toward the north-east. You'll know we're close when we start to climb mountains."

At that time, neither he nor I realized how fortuitous it was that he should make these comments to me.

~

$\mathcal{W}$e were several hours away from Dunladun when we walked straight into Winston's ambush.

Marcelo and I knew we still had a long way to go, and there was nothing to do but put the miles behind us. Marcelo's thoughts distracted him, and the scenery distracted me.

Even once the attack began, several moments passed before I understood what was happening. By then Winston and five of his men had yanked Marcelo off his horse.

Marcelo fell hard. A whoosh of air expelled from his lungs over the sound of startled horses. I watched his head thump against the rocky edge of the roadside.

Winston capitalized upon his brutality, made exponentially worse by the element of surprise. Before Marcelo could shake his head clear of its injury, Winston was upon him. He straddled Marcelo and hit him in the face. I looked on, helpless, as blood streamed from Marcelo's nose.

Winston hit him over and again. The slapping sound of skin against skin and the crunching sound of bone leveling bone made me jump each time. My stomach tied itself into an anguished knot while I reached for thoughts of how I could help.

Marcelo no longer resisted Winston's blows.

I realized, horrified, that he was unconscious.

One of Winston's men placed his hand on his lord's shoulder, preventing him from killing Marcelo, and Winston looked up at him with a depth of fury that I couldn't understand.

The rage ebbed long enough for Winston to bark orders at his henchmen.

Marcelo came to just in time to thrash violently against the men who tightened ropes around his hands and feet. But by then, Marcelo's resistance proved futile. Our attackers tightened the final knots with an audible creaking of ropes that gave all the slack they would ever give.

Marcelo sought me out with wild eyes. Disoriented from the fall, he didn't appear to know which direction to turn to find me. When his eyes finally met mine, it was with desperation. I was now at the mercy of these savage men. He wouldn't be able to help me.

The open road wasn't a safe place for unaccompanied women. I was painfully aware of that. And these weren't just any bandits. Winston was undoubtedly there for me.

If Maggie were in my place, she'd be praying. I tried to think what I should do to protect myself and to free Marcelo. I could do magic—sort of. I might not have any control over it, nor could I anticipate what would happen if I tried, but surely I had to do something.

Winston had resumed beating Marcelo. Horrifically, Marcelo's blood splattered across Winston's face.

Winston seemed to relish his gruesome appearance, and wanted to hurt Marcelo all the more. His men looked on, impassive, and I understood that they must have witnessed Winston's savagery many times before.

Marcelo's eyes weren't on me any longer. They were rolled back in his head, unable to warn me of the danger of discovery if I performed magic.

I was suspended in that frozen moment in time that

passes in a heartbeat toward regret. I needed to do something, no matter the consequences. At this rate, Winston would kill Marcelo soon. I saw no indication that he planned to stop.

And once he eliminated Marcelo, he would turn his attention toward me. I appreciated with a wave of nausea how awful his attention would be. I didn't know if I was his fiancée anymore or if he would care if I was, or if it would matter to him who my father was. A man like this would give into cruelty and have his way with me.

One last look toward Marcelo confirmed the decision I'd already made. His body wasn't reacting to the blows anymore. He was almost lifeless. Soon, it would be too late to save him.

I had no choice.

I let all thought rush from my mind and put aside the panic that threatened to shut me down. I averted my eyes from Marcelo—I couldn't stand to look at what Winston was doing to him—and turned them to nothing in particular. My eyes lost their focus and the sounds of the blows faded.

Then I did what Marcelo had earlier begged me not to do. I allowed my hazy thoughts to drift toward the air's beauty. I felt the crisp air of almost spring against my face, flushed with fright and agitation; the air was cool and refreshing. I noticed my next breath and how the air filled my lungs. It was a precious gift, without any expectation of return on its gesture. My thoughts trailed my exhale.

The breath nourished and restored me; it allowed me to live. Without it, I could not be, nor could anyone else. It was one thing that defined life. A wave of deep admiration coursed through me.

I no longer heard anything at all. I didn't even hear Winston's rallying cries of victory, as if he were courageous for killing an incapacitated man. I tuned out the responding cries of his men, saluting their leader's misguided sense of manliness.

My awareness honed fully into my breath, and I heard and knew nothing but the beauty of the air and all that was contained within one humble breath. That one breath held everything within it.

I didn't even feel the wind caress my hair as its energy began to build, pulling strands loose from my comb. No one paid attention to the breeze then, certainly not Winston or his men.

The wind gathered more strength.

Had Winston and his men looked my way, they might have suspected I was the one doing this.

Thick-stranded red curls whipped around my head like the wild snakes of Medusa.

In that moment, I must have looked like a witch.

But no one saw me for what I was.

The air responded to that part of my mind beyond defined thoughts and revealed its ferocity with suddenness.

A gust of wind strong enough to knock over grown men whipped in the air, building even more force, before blowing directly at Winston and his small troop. Not even a hair rustled on Marcelo's blood-soaked forehead.

At last, Winston realized something unusual was taking place, and so did the horses. Winston had left them tied to trees off the road, and now they revealed their hiding places with anxious cries. Animals could feel extraordinary power more readily than humans.

The horse I was riding, on the other hand, didn't waver. He didn't rear or startle. He weathered the oncoming storm as if he knew I was creating it and that the eye of the storm was the safest place to be. His serenity affected the other three horses that traveled with us, and they too remained calm, unaffected by the ferocious gusts that tore at our attackers.

Luckily, the overwhelming nature of the winds prevented Winston from looking toward me.

It was easy for a man who disparaged women to dismiss the possibilities of their power. That prejudicial thinking would serve me well.

My eyes, however, registered none of it. The air responded immediately to its deeper knowing of me, and it ripped the six men from their roots.

It blew them away.

It was a simple solution for something as powerful as air, and the men faded first to a speck, then to nothing, yanked from the earth as they had yanked Marcelo from his mount moments before, a poetic ending to a vile situation.

I never learned how far the wind carried the men. It took me quite some time to return to myself. When I did, the horses were still, patiently waiting for me as if they were aware of everything that had happened and why.

Perhaps they were.

I looked around me as if waking from a dream, surprised

to discover the visual confirmations of what, deep down somewhere, I recognized as what I had done.

Marcelo was on the ground, discarded in a pool of his own blood.

The sight brought me back to myself faster than anything else could. Within moments, I'd dismounted my horse to rush to him.

"Marcelo," I whispered with more tenderness than I realized I had within me for this man. I wanted to touch his face. But nowhere seemed safe to touch. His face was battered. The handsome features I enjoyed were unrecognizable in a camouflage of color, blood, and the starts of incipient swelling.

I watched his chest, and I didn't realize I'd been holding my breath until it all rushed out in relief. Marcelo's chest had risen and fallen. He was breathing. He was still alive, but I couldn't tell how long he'd stay that way. Whenever any serious injuries occurred at Norland Manor, Mother or Father promptly ordered my sisters and me away. It was not a sight for ladies, they told us. As a consequence, I had scant experience with wounds, especially any as severe as Marcelo's.

I looked around. We were alone on an isolated stretch of road. I could see no homesteads ahead or behind us. Driven to the road by Winston in the first place, we had none of our usual things with us. There was nothing for me to rummage through to see if I could find something that would help.

I was alone with an unconscious, almost-dead magician,

with only horses as company, in a man's world, dangerous for women.

I suddenly felt very much like an inadequate girl and wanted nothing more than to crumble and cry at my ill fortune.

But even amidst the temptation, I wouldn't.

When I rose from Marcelo's side, I left the inadequate girl behind and rose a woman.

SOMETHING VERY MUCH LIKE MAGIC

I didn't know how long we had before Winston and his men would be able to pursue us again. Regardless, Marcelo didn't have any time to spare. I had to get moving right away.

I told the horses to stay put and to take care of Marcelo. I said it to comfort myself, to help me feel that I wasn't all alone in this. But as I walked away, the horses shifted slightly toward Marcelo. I looked back, surprised, but continued to move.

I arrived at Winston's hidden horses quickly. They were surprisingly calm now, and I untied each horse from his tree without any problem. I retied each horse to his neighbor, until the six could follow one another in a line and, together, we returned to Marcelo.

I'd never seen ten horses as docile as these when close to one another, and I was able to tie them all together so they could follow the horse I rode. However, arranging ten horses under the guidance of one rider was the lesser of my problems. How would I be able to lift Marcelo onto a horse? He was taller than me, broader than me, and at present, he was dead weight.

My mind drew blanks as it searched for possibilities. If I knew how to control my magic, the feat of lifting Marcelo onto a horse could be easy. But I had no idea how to do it. I didn't even know where to begin, and I feared hurting Marcelo even more with my lack of experience. He couldn't afford any further injury.

I looked at my horse in desperation. I had plenty of horses to carry Marcelo. I just couldn't get him onto one.

Then something incredible happened. I'd ridden horses most of my life, yet I'd never seen something like this before. It was enough to convince me that magic—or something very much like it—existed.

My horse advanced a few steps toward me, suggesting that each horse behind him follow. They lined up next to the body. Then Marcelo's horse, the second behind mine, drew parallel to his limp form.

Like the domesticated camels of the Far East Father's friends told stories about, Marcelo's horse lowered himself to the ground, bending his knees under him.

I watched the horse, incredulous, until I found myself blinking away tears. My heart leapt. Like this, I was certain I could get Marcelo onto his horse.

"Oh, thank you," I said, now more certain than ever that the horses would understand me.

With as much care as I could, I lifted Marcelo from under his arms and dragged him closer to the horse. I pulled some more until Marcelo's upper body sat against the horse, his feet straight out in front of him.

I hadn't thought how to keep an unconscious Marcelo from slipping off his horse once he was on it. Should I put him on his stomach or on his back? I decided I needed to protect his face, which had taken most of the beating, instead of allowing it to bounce against the horse with each stride.

I shoved and pulled until Marcelo's waist curved around the horse's back.

I scavenged through the saddlebags of Winston's horses until I found another length of rope and a knife. The rope was long enough to cut in half, and I tied Marcelo's hands to the left stirrup and his feet to the right. I hoped that would be enough to secure him as I stepped back to inspect my work.

I wasn't convinced it would work, so I rearranged the ties between the horses so that his horse would ride next to mine. I'd have to watch him, and maybe even hold onto him, as we made our way.

Even though I was fully unnerved by the precariousness of the transport situation, I knew that what I had come up with would have to do. Marcelo was still bleeding, and he hadn't moved once, not even while I dragged him atop a horse.

"You can get up now," I told Marcelo's horse.

I held onto Marcelo's body while his horse slowly rose, aware of the care he needed to have with his cargo.

I put my hand on the horse's nose while I thanked him, but it seemed insufficient. I brought my forehead to his and felt the heat of his nostrils on my neck. "Thank you," I said again, and this time it felt right.

I walked to my horse, mounted, and set us all off at a slow pace. I monitored Marcelo. Besides bouncing unpleasantly, he seemed to be doing all right with the movement.

He continued to bleed from deep gashes on his head. Winston struck him wearing heavy family rings that gouged his flesh.

I picked up the pace as much as I dared, and we rode—a limp body, ten horses, and me—toward the first homestead we could find.

A VALIANCE WITHOUT SIZE

*I*t was mid-afternoon before I found a place to stop. Winston had attacked us on an isolated stretch of road. Had there been more choices—or any other choice at all—I would have passed this farm by.

It was rundown, though smoke exited the chimney. There were several corrals for animals, without an animal in sight. In fact, the farm was unusually quiet, and that made me nervous. The crunching sound of gravel under hooves rang out loudly against the surrounding silence as we made our way down the long, narrow road toward the farmstead.

My horse pricked his ears back against his head as if he, too, felt something out of place. Our wariness slowed our pace automatically. As we grew closer, I noticed that the windows were shuttered and the gates and doors closed.

I almost turned back.

But one look at Marcelo and the open gashes on his head convinced me to urge the horses forward. We plodded on.

Other than the steady trail of smoke that floated skyward, the farmhouse appeared abandoned. I edged the horses toward the gate that led to the house itself and pointed them back toward the road. I also left them untied, in case we had to leave quickly. After how the horses behaved with Marcelo, I was less worried about their running off than I was about approaching the house.

I got down from my horse, patting him on the neck. "I'll be right back," I told him.

I could feel his stare and that of all the other horses on my back as I reached a hand to open the wooden gate. When the gate hinges creaked loudly, I could feel the horses' apprehension mirroring my own. Still, there was nothing I could do about any of it. Without treatment soon, Marcelo would die.

The steps it took me to reach the front door of the rickety-looking house seemed to pass too fast. Before I knew it, I was there, swallowing my nerves yet again, raising my hand to knock on the door.

However, my hand never made contact with the wooden door. It never made a sound.

Even if it had, I wouldn't have heard it over the screaming and banging that came from inside the house.

I couldn't tell what it was. It sounded like war cries, cursing, and pots banging, all at once. The racket was intended to scare me off and, had I not been desperate, it probably would have.

Instead, I rose my voice so whoever was inside would hear me over the ruckus.

"I don't mean any harm. Please. I just need some help."

The din didn't abate. My heart sank until I realized that the noise would have to stop at some point, and I could try again then.

I waited. The noise continued heartily.

Until it didn't.

The cries grew hoarse, the banging less enthusiastic.

Finally, it ceased all together.

"Please. My friend will die if you don't help me."

Still, nothing.

"I have a few coins I can give you," I said, though I had none. Marcelo did, however. Somewhere.

The silence grew deafening. I could almost hear consideration of my offer taking place on the other side of the door.

Then there was another creaking sound, and the front door opened less than an inch, only enough for one brown eye to study me. The height of the eye was that of a man, but even the sliver of face I could see told me otherwise.

"You're safe with me. I promise. My friend over there was attacked by riders."

While I pointed toward Marcelo's limp form, the door inched open another sliver.

"I need to do something to help him. Please."

The sigh that came from the other side of the door was loud enough for me to hear it. Then, the scuffing of a chair dragged across the floor. More sounds of furniture moving followed. He'd barricaded the door.

When the door finally opened, a boy of no more than eight or nine looked out at me.

"Ya can never be too careful. Travelers be dangerous."

I strained my ears to understand him. His speech was fast and sloppy, that of someone who had never received the tutelage of governesses as I had.

"Yes, I know that very well. Thank you very much for opening the door."

"Ya," he said, and a mop of brown, scraggly hair bounced as he nodded.

The interior of the house was dark and dank, dirty and messy. It didn't look like anyone was keeping house.

"Are you here alone?"

I watched as he puffed up his scraggy chest and prepared to tell me a lie. But his chest quickly deflated, along with his spirit. "Ya, I'm all alone here."

I didn't know what a boy younger than me could do to help Marcelo. Yet there wasn't enough time to find some-place else. It had already taken me too long to find this one.

"My friend is badly hurt. I don't know what to do to help him," I said.

"Can we get him inside? Me ma used to nurse people. Her medicines are all here."

Unencumbered by fears now, the boy had exited the house and was moving toward Marcelo.

He gave a low whistle. "We need to move him. Ya can't hang him upside down like this fa long. He's dripping blood. We need to get him off the horse. Hold on," he said and ran off.

By the time he returned with the wheelbarrow, I'd directed Marcelo's horse to lower himself to the ground again. Just like before, he did so gracefully, taking care not to jostle his rider.

A look of surprise swept across the boy's face, but just as quickly, it was gone.

"Let's move him," he said while he positioned the wheelbarrow by the kneeling horse. The height was perfect.

I untied Marcelo's feet and hands. Then the boy pulled while I pushed, and we got Marcelo's body into the wheelbarrow.

The boy was already leading the pushcart toward the house when I leaned over to Marcelo's horse.

"Thank you," I said again. I heard the horse begin to stand back up as I ran toward the house. I followed the boy in.

The house was worse off than it had looked from the outside. It needed a good wipe down and a sweeping. The boy had left the wheelbarrow with Marcelo in it next to the dining table. He was busy clearing crusty dishes from it. I walked over to help, following his lead and piling the dishes on a side table.

Once clear, the boy looked at me. "Ready?"

I looked at the cart. I looked at the table. "The table's too high. We won't be able to lift him up, just the two of us. Why not the floor?"

"Nah. Floor's cold."

He and I looked around.

"We could push together a few chairs. They're the right height," I said.

"Aye. Ya're right."

We unfurled Marcelo from the contortion the wheel-barrow forced on him, then pulled and shoved until we stretched him out onto the chairs. He hadn't moved since Winston knocked him out.

The boy rushed off to procure the medicines we needed. I heard him jostling glass bottles in the next room. Then he came running out. He placed three bottles of different sizes on the table and then returned for more.

When he was finished, he lined up five bottles of dark tinctures and potions. I didn't know how to use a single one.

"Please tell me you know how to use these."

"Aye. I do."

A rush of premature relief swept through me. "Oh, thank goodness."

"I helped me ma a lot. She told me I had to know how to take care of meself. Looks like me ma was right."

A look of sadness threatened to descend upon him before he quickly tucked it away. "There's a bucket of clean water over there. Bring it to me."

It went like that. Me following Carl's orders—I finally asked his name—while I watched him in admiration. Meticulously, he cleaned Marcelo's wounds. There were many of them, and he took his time with each one.

First, he wiped the caked and fresh blood away with water. Then, he poured some kind of tincture on the wounds. He didn't tell me what things were as he used them. He was too focused to bother with conversation, other than to tell me that it was lucky Marcelo was still asleep. These tinctures stung, he told me with the look of a boy who'd tumbled and fallen plenty in his short life.

While Marcelo's wounds absorbed the medicines, Carl looked around the house. "If ya're going to be on the road with him, ya'll need to bandage the cuts so they don't go bad. But I don't think I have any clean cloths in the house."

I didn't imagine he did. Nothing in the house looked clean.

I looked down at my dress. It wasn't that clean either, but it would have to do. I tore the underskirt into strips, and Carl disinfected them by soaking them in the medicine he'd poured on Marcelo's open wounds.

"I don't have any more food here. We'll need to keep on even though it would be better for him not to travel. I don't see how it can be helped."

"*We* will need to keep going?"

"Ya. Take me with you."

I couldn't imagine taking on any more responsibility than I had. Already, it was more than I could handle.

But before he even said please, the look in his eyes had convinced me. I couldn't leave him there, alone, unfed, and unclean.

Again, I was backed into a space of no choice. I had to do the right thing.

"All right. Come with us. But only until I find a safe place for you."

Carl looked crestfallen, tired of having so little control over the outcome of his life.

"It's not that I don't want you along," I continued. "It's just that the men who did this to him are still after us. You'll be in danger if you stay with us. I need to leave you some-place safe, away from these men. Do you understand?"

"I guess."

"Do you have water for the horses?"

"Ya. There's a well at the edge of the corrals, and watering troughs there too."

"All right. I'll go water the horses. You prepare to leave as soon as possible."

The sun was already sinking lower in the sky as I stepped out of the house, and by the time I came back, Carl was ready. He'd put on a battered coat and worn shoes and packed a kit of his mother's medicines in a basket, the glass bottles padded with worn linen he tore into pieces.

"Before we leave, I wanna show you something. I put ointment on his chest to ward the fever since he isn't awake to drink any medicine. And look." He lifted Marcelo's shirt. "Y'ever seen scars like these before?"

I stared, wide-eyed, at a criss-cross weaving of scar tissue across an otherwise normal chest. "No," I said, stunned.

What traumas marked Marcelo's past? It shook me to realize I had no idea.

We struggled to figure out a better way to transport Marcelo, but discovered none. We had no carriage or even a wagon. In the end, we strapped Marcelo back onto his horse just as I'd done before. Then we set off toward the next town over. According to Carl, it was less than an hour away. If we were lucky, we would manage to avoid all people and bandits and make it just before sundown.

A GENTLE STOP ON A LONG ROAD

*L*uck was on our side after all, just not in the way we'd imagined it would be. Not far from Carl's abandoned farmstead, a horse and buggy drew near us.

Carl and I exchanged alarmed looks. We were a defenseless young woman and boy, with an injured man who could do nothing to protect us, along with the tangible wealth of ten horses. We were at the mercy of whoever crossed our path.

It was useless to turn off the road and hide. We'd spotted the oncomer too late. If we ran, he would just follow us and make a bad situation potentially worse.

We continued forward, trying to remain calm. My horse sensed my nerves and reacted to how I felt by blowing hot air from his nostrils. It reminded me to hold it together.

I focused on keeping my breathing even and slow, but I was careful not to focus on it too much. I didn't want to rouse the air.

The buggy reached us. Its driver pulled his horse to a stop.

"Where you kids going with all those horses?" the man asked us. He was big and burly, with a bushy beard and thick hair ruffled by the journey. Though Carl and I wore coats, the man wore shirtsleeves rolled up to expose brawny muscles.

"We were traveling with my friend when some men attacked us. My friend hasn't woken up since. He was hurt pretty badly."

The man looked toward Marcelo. He didn't have to inspect him closely to see that what I said was plausible. Marcelo's head and face were one bandage after another, and the skin that showed in between was already brutally discolored.

"And where are ya headed?"

"My friend and I," I said while pointing to Marcelo's body, "are headed to Irele. And Carl's with us until we find him someplace safe to stay."

"I see. Well, the next town over's only about half an hour away. That's where I come from. I'll head back with you, and we'll figure how to help you there."

He eyed us. "My missus is handy with the medicines. And I suppose we can find you a bed to sleep in and a place to put up the horses for the night."

I felt the whoosh of relief sweep through Carl as readily as it did through me.

"That would be wonderful, sir. I'd be very grateful to you. We really need the help."

"Yes, I see that." The man stepped down from his buggy and went over to Marcelo. "You kids fix him up like this?"

"I did. Me ma taught me how."

"You did a good job, son. But you can't keep this man like this. We need to move him to my cart."

He began to untie Marcelo's hands and feet, while I hoped he was as nice as he seemed. There wasn't much I could do to help Marcelo if it were otherwise. I stayed on my horse and watched the man sling Marcelo over his shoulder with ease. He deposited Marcelo in his cart with more gentleness than I could have hoped for, and we were off again.

The man turned his horse back, and we journeyed toward his home.

~

It turned out that the man and his wife were kind. They put Marcelo, Carl, and me all up for the night in their home above the family bakery; the man carried Marcelo up the stairs across his back.

We slept on blankets on the floor in front of the hearth, and I was grateful for the meager accommodations. They didn't have room for the horses, but a neighbor did.

The missus treated Marcelo's wounds and put fresh bandages on them. She said she thought there was a good chance he would make it, as long as the fever didn't set in.

Once the strain of the day was finally over and it was time to rest, I fell into a dreamless sleep, and I didn't stir until the smells of fresh baked bread wafted up through the fireplace.

I couldn't find the man and his wife once I got up. Carl was still sleeping, and Marcelo hadn't shifted at all in the night. So I laced my shoes and went down the stairs into the back of the bakery.

By the time Carl woke, the husband and his wife had offered to keep Carl with them. The woman was barren, frustrating their desire for a son. Carl was young enough that he could easily become a part of their family and help in the bakery. Once he cleaned up, they were sure Carl would be able to do his part in the family business.

I raided Marcelo's pockets until I found a pouch that bore the Count of Norland's crest outlined in cracked fragments of red wax. I had seen the seal so many times before; I didn't have to piece it together to be sure.

I gave to the family generously, for their kindness and to help support Carl for a little while, and though they were surprised at first, they accepted it. Times were difficult for those of lesser means.

When I made my way out of town early that morning, my horse and Marcelo's pulled the man's buggy, and eight horses trailed behind it. It was an uncommon sight for certain, a young girl sitting in the driver's seat with an unconscious man in a cart.

I hoped no one would notice the oddity as I pointed the entourage northeast. The family didn't know exactly where Irele was, but they were certain it connected to this road.

I squinted my eyes against the rising sun and settled in. It was going to be a long ride.

HOPE FLIES TOWARD IRELE

hree days had passed since I said my farewells to Carl, and already I was overcome with worry. I had been fortunate enough to find inconspicuous lodging for my unconscious companion and myself for two nights—something that I hadn't known if I'd be able to do—and now I hoped to arrive in Irele before nightfall.

Still, my mind was ill at ease. Marcelo had finally begun to move, although now I almost wished he hadn't. His eyes remained fixedly closed—they had not opened once—while he moaned and writhed in discomfort.

The fever had set in.

Carl's new mother's warning echoed through my mind, though I tried to shoo it away: "He'll likely survive as long as his body doesn't fall into fever." Well, his body had. I didn't even have to touch him to know that he was burning up from the inside. Sweat coated his face, soaked his hairline, and beaded up on his forehead and upper lip, where it was visible even among the stubble that shadowed his face.

Marcelo didn't respond when I spoke to him. He seemed only to react to the pain that held him captive. I had attempted to spoon feed him water multiple times, but I couldn't get him to open his parched, cracked lips.

He lay in the cart, where I had made him as comfortable as possible. But he rejected all my efforts to help him.

As the fever sucked him further into its depths, I had begun to wonder whether I would lose him. The thought brought forth a deep sense of loss—I cried for the possible death of a man I had never called a friend, but now suspected had become one just the same.

All the while, the horses continued their progress toward the northeast. I hoped beyond all hope that we would arrive in Irele soon.

But I wasn't sure. I'd consulted few people, not wanting to bring attention to my situation, but no one had known exactly where Irele was. Several had heard of it, but they only knew it was to the northeast somewhere. Like the baker, they could give me no more direction than to follow this road and hope I would run into it soon.

I rode while time stretched and distorted. There was nothing to distract me from Marcelo's maddening groans. The clop-clop-clop of horses that I normally enjoyed proved grating. I could do nothing more to help Marcelo. I had already tended to his wounds that day with medicine from the baker's wife, and that was all I knew to do. The danger was now greater from the fever than from the swollen and discolored wounds that marred his face and head.

I moved slowly toward Irele.

The sun was high overhead. Sweat trickled down the curve of my back beneath my buttoned coat. My hair was once more knotted and matted despite Marcelo's gift of the comb, which I hadn't used since Winston attacked us.

My face was sunburned, but I didn't care as I stared at the sun, wary of its eventual setting. I had to reach Irele before sundown today. If not, I felt in my heart that Marcelo would not make it. Any delay now would seal Marcelo's fate, and he would die.

The faintest breeze swirled up the mountain, urging me along as it went. And on this breeze, hope flew.

I shielded my eyes to see better, to make sure it was not a mirage brought on by my desperation. There, so far away that it was only a silhouette, was what looked like a fortress. It stood, even in miniature, strong and impenetrable, and I knew then that this was Albacus and Mordecai's stronghold.

I was approaching Irele. I would get Marcelo to Albacus and Mordecai's estate before nightfall. Marcelo's chances of survival strengthened, just by the proximity to Irele and the miracle for which I hoped.

"We're close," I told my horse and Marcelo's. "We're going to the fortress on that mountain side. Now ride as fast as you can. The magician's life depends on it."

I didn't have to shake their reins. They knew what to do like I did. The horses took off at a constrained gallop, because the cart would not stand up to more.

I looked back. Marcelo was strapped in. I had wrapped cloth scraps around his wrists and ankles so the ties that bound him to the cart would not tear at his flesh as they rubbed against him. I left little berth for movement, minimizing Marcelo's bouncing as much as I could. Now I was relieved that I had.

The horses raced along, Marcelo at their mercy. And it was because of mercy that they rode as fiercely as they did. The discomfort the fever caused was far worse and far more worrying than the eventual soreness his body would suffer from the speed of travel.

He had a chance now, greater than he'd had since Winston first cocked his fist back while aiming it at a handsome face. Now, I willed that Albacus and Mordecai, or at least one of them, were home. If they were not, it would have all been in vain.

Marcelo would die in Irele.

AN UNEXPECTED FAIRY TALE ENDING

$\mathcal{B}$y the time the road began to weave its way upward, the horses were tired. They had ridden hard and valiantly, doing their part to save Marcelo's life.

I was exhausted even before we began the day's trek.

But we couldn't stop.

Not now.

Not when the fortress was finally within sight. "I know you're tired," I told my horse and Marcelo's, the ones in the lead. "But we must keep going. We're almost there."

The horses blew out hot breath, gathered what strength they had, and tilted their heads into the rising incline.

But as I looked up I realized we weren't almost there, not really.

The fortress appeared to be almost straight up from where we were. The horses kicked at loose rocks as they climbed, and the rocks went tumbling downhill behind them.

Marcelo hung at an incline, tied to the cart. I hoped he

would make it up the mountain. After all our combined effort, it would be terrible to lose him now. He looked worse than I'd seen him these last few days. It was hard to tell from where I sat, but it seemed as if his breathing had grown shallow, the fever a beast out of control.

I turned forward again, determination rising within me as rapidly as the fever was consuming the magician. I felt ready to get out of the cart to push it, to do something to help us move faster. I'd grown tired of feeling helpless.

Because I lived in a man's world, I'd always felt limited. I was born in the shadow of a boy, my deceased brother. Then, external circumstances and everyone I encountered made me painfully aware of all that a young woman wasn't supposed to do.

No one was around to stop me now. From where I sat, directing the cart right behind the two horses, I did not spot a human or animal anywhere. The limits I felt constrained by now were all my own, the residue of years of observing others restrict me.

I might not be able to contribute physically to our slow-yet-steady progress up the mountain, but perhaps there was something else I could do.

I studied the steep incline. It might take us hours to climb the mountain to reach the fortress that punctuated its summit. The horses' breath was already labored, their muscles taut as they toiled and worked. Sweat dampened their coats, and froth was beginning to build at the corner of my horse's mouth.

This would not do. The horses had worked hard enough

to help us. They had become our partners in this journey. My heart sank at their suffering.

I should do something to help them and to help Marcelo.

Suddenly, I knew what to do. The idea came seemingly from nowhere. Yet there it was, strong and undeniable.

I wouldn't dismiss it.

I could not. To do so would be to deny the person I was becoming.

Our predicament was bringing clarity and alacrity where there had been none before. Suddenly, the worry fell away. The sounds of the struggling horses blended into the background, behind my rapidly pulsing thoughts. Marcelo drifted away in the distance, much farther behind me than his bindings would allow.

The sun stood still, its descent toward the horizon frozen along with time. I was no longer in any hurry.

I turned toward Albacus and Mordecai's fortress. Details of the brothers' estate came into focus. I could make out the entrance to the fortress now. My eyes bore down on the gate as if I could transport myself to that very spot by will alone.

I understood what I needed to do, and I had decided to do it. With the first flash of knowing, I'd chosen to do what I'd never done before: to step beyond any boundaries, even those that were self-imposed.

My gaze bore down on the entrance to the fortress as if the intensity of it could get us there. Perhaps it could some-day; I didn't know. But not today. Today, I took my thoughts someplace else.

My eyes began to blur, and I recognized the familiarity

of the process, even though I had only done this a few times. I'd introduced myself to the element of air before—or perhaps it was the air that had introduced itself to me—and I could already feel that air and I were no longer strangers.

At first it was just a whistle of the wind, skipping across the road behind me, as if it were the most innocent of things. But this time, I had chosen to use magic on a grander scale than an experiment from *The Magyke of the Elementes*. Now, I was stepping into my power, or at least what little I understood of it.

The whistle behind me grew louder as it amassed more substance. The air's desire to fully expose its power grew in bursts, and I realized in an instant that I did not control the element of air. It could not be controlled, not by me or anyone else—not truly at least. Air could pretend; it could give off the appearance that a magician dominated it. But that would never be so.

Then, I comprehended one of the most important lessons I would ever come to learn of magic. The elements —air, earth, water, and fire—were bigger than any one human mind.

Life would cease to exist without them.

There was no controlling or manipulating them as *The Magyke of Elementes* suggested. The elements *allowed* me to interact with them, to suggest what I might like them to do. They indulged me because they wanted to, because they enjoyed the process.

And as I approached the air with respect and reverence for its innate power, the air was content. It wanted to play with me, to see what would happen next, just as I did.

What had been a whistle expanded. The slight breeze transformed into a sharp gust, strong enough to contribute energy to the horses' efforts. The horses continued uphill, noticing with their next steps that their tiresome trudging was less burdensome.

The current increased, concentrating more of the air's almost unlimited energy within it. The horses' steps grew lighter. Thus, the horses' spirits did too.

My eyes saw nothing anymore, not even the colored shape of the brothers' estate. I'd already shared my intention with the air. There was no need to think of it any longer. I let my eyelids drop the rest of the way down.

I was tapping into a small bit of my mind's potential. But it was more than I'd done before, and the part of me that I'd restrained reveled in its newly found freedom.

Within myself, I delved into the air that swirled through me as much as it did around me. I joined it.

Just as quickly as I let all thoughts of control go, the air picked up Marcelo and me, ten horses, and a cart as easily as if we were the seeds of cotton floating on a pleasant zephyr. The horses continued lifting their legs at first, until they surrendered to the uncomfortable feeling that they did not touch dirt. Every horse looked down to either side, unnerved by the lack of visible support beneath.

Like the most magical of carriages in the fairy tales Gertrude, my other sisters, and I had read around hearths, we floated and flew. The air current wound us up the steep roadway, the precipices that broke off to the sides nothing more than a pretty view.

When I opened my eyes again, my heart leapt with joy. I

was experiencing true magic now. This was better than Cinderella's pumpkin-turned-carriage, and it was better than Saint Nicholas' flying sled. I was intimately connected to this. I was living the magic. I was the princess of the fairy tale, and the wind swept me off my feet in wonderful accommodating fashion. I was the princess, on her way to save the prince, flying to Merlin's castle.

The air rose and climbed, as we did along with it. Trees that perched and clung wildly to rocky mountainsides and overhangs were a blur as we passed. A frigid waterfall plummeted through a crevice, its overpowering rushing sound providing the ideal thematic music as we circled it.

By the time the air escorted us to the very top, to the very pinnacle of that rocky, nearly perpendicular mountain, I felt like a true princess, and I believed that everything had to go right in my fairy tale now. It had all been too magical for any other result.

So when we came to a stop at the gate to the fortress— once the air had flown away to take part in another adventure, stillness replacing it—I was completely unprepared for the two grumpy-looking men that worked to open the monumental wooden gate.

The brothers didn't look like any fairy tale ending I could imagine.

AN UNCERTAIN FUTURE

"I told you it was someone young and inexperienced," said the brother with the longest beard I'd ever seen. His beard was braided, and even so, it reached past his waist.

"Yes, but you can't deny there is power in her. So my conclusion was perfectly justifiable," the other brother said. His long hair was braided into perhaps hundreds of thin braids, like I'd seen women wear in engravings from Father's books of exotic islands. The beads at the end of each braid clinked together, rustling when he moved.

The brothers finished heaving a gate open that was several times taller than them, and now they walked toward me.

"It's curious that she should come today. The runes said all life would change on this day. And now here she is, a surprise visitor," Long Beard said. I couldn't know which of the brothers was Albacus and which was Mordecai. Marcelo had told me almost nothing about them.

"Yes, it's curious indeed. But that doesn't mean that she's the catalyst of change. Her arrival could be coincidence and nothing more," Beaded Hair said, and Long Beard barked out laughter so loud that it startled me.

The brothers continued their approach as if I weren't a real person, right there, listening to every word they said.

"As if you believed in coincidence! You're the one who always tells me there's no such thing, that the entire universe moves to create points of actions that cross and come together," Long Beard said, his braided beard still shaking from laughter.

"Yes, well, I suppose you're right on this one point." Braided Hair made eye contact with me for the first time. "We shall have to see how this plays out," he said, looking me straight in the eyes. But neither he nor his brother stopped their progress to speak with me. They were interested in my cargo and stopped only once they reached the cart.

"I thought it might be him, though I'd dearly hoped it wouldn't be," Braided Hair said.

"He's in grave danger," Long Beard said without even reaching out to touch Marcelo. His conclusion was apparent to anyone with an acute mind and good eyesight, and the brothers seemed to possess both despite their age. They walked without the typical curved spines of the elderly, but their hair was gray as dust.

I spun in my seat at the front of the cart to watch as the brothers pulled themselves into the wagon. They sat, dangling their legs over the edge. They swung their legs and feet contentedly, and it struck me as a disorienting sight for old men to act as children when it was clear that there was an emergency. Marcelo stretched across the line between life and death within arm's reach of them, and I had thought that both men cared about him.

Long Beard reached his arm back without turning around and snapped his fingers in the direction of the horses. He did it with such a casual lack of concern that I was shocked when the horses responded immediately. The horses walked through the gate.

I continued to watch as Long Beard motioned one hand toward the open gate as easily as if he were brushing a fly away. The gate pulled shut behind us.

I blinked and opened my eyes wider. I had never seen magic done like this before, and I wondered why the brothers hadn't opened the gate this way to begin with.

The horses came to a halt in front of the entrance to the castle, exactly where Long Beard wanted them. My head was still turned to watch the brothers. I didn't want to miss a second of what seemed like a performance. They hopped off the cart with a youthful vitality that befuddled me. I had never seen anything like it before.

The brothers began to walk toward the castle when Braided Hair twisted the fingers of one hand in the air. I watched, still amazed, as the ropes I'd tied with such precision and care unwound themselves on their own. Then Braided Hair flattened the same hand as if he were carrying a tray, and Marcelo's body lifted into the air and followed the brothers, hovering.

Braided Hair guided the man I understood to be their pupil into the darkness of the castle. The front door opened for them, and the brothers disappeared within with Marcelo's limp body.

I remained seated where I was. I didn't know what to do. I had done nothing more than swivel my head to follow the brothers since they first exited the gate.

They had not acknowledged me other than to speak of me. They certainly hadn't invited me to follow them in. I sat there, perplexed, until a man finally came out from a building adjacent to the castle to care for the horses.

"Go," he said. "They'll be expecting you inside."

So I stepped down from the cart and walked on unsteady limbs toward an uncertain future.

ONE OF A KIND

*I*t was lucky for me that I'd been too concerned with Marcelo and how to get to Irele to formulate any expectations, because if I had, the interior of the castle would have immediately dashed them away.

Unlike Norland Manor, the castle was dark even during daylight. Candles adorned most flat surfaces to illuminate what an overhead chandelier didn't. The candlelight cast eerie shadows across the walls and crawled across strange artifacts I couldn't readily identify.

I looked around. There was no sign of the brothers or of anyone else. Reluctantly, I returned to the front door and closed it. Spring was not quite here yet, and the chill of the approaching night, combined with the higher altitude, would create the kind of cold that penetrates to the bone. As soon as the door latched closed, I yearned for the fading daylight the open door had allowed in.

Perhaps it was more the stage in my life before magic had entered it that I yearned for, when things had seemed easier and safe though stifling and stagnant. When I closed that door, I understood that I was closing the door on my past forever. By stepping inside the castle and leaving behind the world outside, I was choosing to accept a part of me that involved both danger and potential in equal measure.

I turned and walked fully into the foyer, rubbing each hand along its opposite arm to warm myself. The undergarments, dress, and coat I wore were insufficient to ward off the cold of high mountains. These stone fortresses retained the cold all winter long. I knew this well from Norland Manor, where I dreaded the coming of winter every year, mourning the passing of fall like the death of a dear friend. But whereas in Norland Manor fires burned throughout the winter in every hearth, I could not spot a single fire from where I stood. The only flames were those of candles.

Even the sound of the closing door had not brought anyone to me. I heard no echoing steps across the stone floors. I saw no movement, even among the shadows, which crowded across the foyer as if they possessed life.

I stepped into the entry hall. It was wide and hinted at the grandness of the castle, of what it could perhaps be if it were lit and allowed vitality.

"Hello!" I said to the empty room and heard my voice bounce off every surface that surrounded me. My voice echoed out of the entry hall until I couldn't hear it any longer, but I thought it might continue throughout the castle like a crashing ocean wave that filled every crevice until, simply, it dispersed into nothingness.

No one came. No voice responded to my call. No

rushing footsteps pattered across cold stone floors to reach me.

I walked toward a tapestry that hung across a wall. Even the candlelight around it did nothing to force its image out from hiding. Already I felt as if this were a castle that contained and hid a great many secrets.

I stepped right next to the tapestry and looked up. It towered and stretched above me. I could barely make out the intertwined legs of humans and animals.

I reached for a candle, and as I moved it toward the tapestry, I noticed something peculiar. The candlestick had no wax drips along its sides. I studied the flame. No liquid wax pooled around it. I ran a finger across the flame. There was no heat.

I held my hand above the flame, steadily. The flame in the candle was as cool as the breezes that howled throughout the castle. I began to understand how the brothers could have so many candles burning at once. Ordinary candles burned quickly and were a valuable commodity.

I picked up a second candle and held both right up to the tapestry, now without fear that the flame would singe it.

I gasped and faltered, taking a step back. What looked like a demonic satyr, with the telltale legs of a goat, held, against her will, a young woman with flowing blonde hair that only partially covered her nude body. The satyr grinned with sadistic pleasure at those who had the distinct *dis*pleasure of viewing this tapestry.

"It's an unpleasant image, that one."

I dropped the candles with a crash and spun to find

Long Beard behind me. I hadn't heard him approach, and I was accustomed to the sounds of steps across stone floors. How had he crept up on me?

I scrambled to pick up the candles from the floor, embarrassed to discover that both candlesticks had shattered. I began to scoop up the ceramic pieces as best as I could.

"I… I'm sorry. You startled me."

"Leave it be, child. We have more important things to tend to."

But I continued to pick up the pieces, more quickly now so as to appear to comply with Long Beard's request. I felt uncomfortable leaving ceramic shards on the floor for someone else to step on.

Long Beard sighed loudly. Then the shards and splinters of porcelain drew together. I snapped my head up to see how he was doing it. He held both hands in front of him as if they held a large imaginary bowl, and he moved them in toward each other. When I looked back down, the fragments had pieced themselves back together.

"Now, will you get up, child?"

I nodded quickly and stood, one candlestick in each hand. I found Long Beard studying me.

"You have questions." It was a statement, and I imagined an obvious one. Of course I had questions. I had so many!

"We don't have much time now, but you may ask what's most pressing."

I hated to squander a question on this, but curiosity nagged at me. "If you consider the tapestry an unpleasant image, why do you hang it here in the entry hall where you'll often see it?"

My question surprised him. "I've never thought to move it from where it is. My great-great-grandfather hung it here, and it hasn't been moved since."

Long Beard looked at the tapestry again. "He was a dark magician. He amassed a valuable collection of dark art."

Involuntarily, I shivered at the thought of more art like this displayed throughout the castle. I was for once grateful that the castle was not better illuminated. I didn't want to see the brothers' ancestral collection of valuable dark art.

"Is that all you need to ask me now?"

I recognized humor in Long Beard's voice, and I thought a barely visible smirk bent his mouth.

I couldn't tell if he was poking fun in a way that bothered me or not, so I decided to hurry on and take advantage of what might be a rare opportunity. There were many concerns that pressed on me, begging for relief.

"Will Marcelo be all right? Will he recover? He's been very ill. I've been terribly worried about him."

Long Beard smiled at me pleasantly, and I decided that he hadn't been mocking me before. His braided beard jiggled as he spoke. "Chances are very good that Marcelo will ultimately come out of this well. Mordecai is with him now. He's a very skilled herbalist and magician of the healing arts. Just don't ever let him know I told you that." A mischievous twinkle skipped across his eyes.

"Is Marcelo awake then?"

"Oh no, not yet. As you say, he's been quite ill. His situation is still grave. The fever has a firm hold on him, and it's reluctant to relinquish its power. But I know my brother well. I feel confident in saying that he'll help Marcelo through this. Mordecai doesn't lack motivation. Marcelo is like a son to him. He'll do all he can to help him and, rest assured, that's quite a lot.

"Don't worry about Marcelo any longer. You can put him out of your mind. You'll see him again once he's healed, but that may be quite some time. No need to waste your mind thinking about him.

"I do, however, thank you for bringing him to us. Had you not, he'd be dead now. That's a certainty. My brother would have been very sad. He can't afford to lose another one."

It seemed that every question Albacus answered sparked more within me, and now I wondered if he was dismissing me. Had he thanked me for bringing Marcelo to Irele to insinuate that they no longer required my presence here?

"Do you want me to leave now?" I asked, hoping hard that he wouldn't say yes. As much as the castle made me uncomfortable and as far away as I was from everything I was familiar with, I didn't want to go out all alone into a world that might not welcome me as a part of it anymore.

"Goodness, no, child."

I was certain my relief was visible.

"We're only just beginning," Albacus said.

Beginning what exactly? I wondered. But before I could ask, I remembered something that had floated around the periphery of my awareness while I aimed for Irele, vying for my attention. It was as bothersome as an insistent fly, but I was too absorbed by worry and weariness to give it the focus it wanted.

"Why didn't Marcelo do magic to save himself from our attackers? Why did he allow himself to be beaten so severely? Why didn't he do something, anything at all? He's a magician, isn't he? Why didn't he do magic when he needed to most?"

"Oh yes, Marcelo's a magician. A very good one too. If Marcelo didn't use magic to ward off your attackers, there must have been a good reason for it. I can think of a few possibilities, but to save you from the ponderings of an old man, it may be easier if you tell me what happened."

I didn't want to bore Albacus with dramatic details I doubted would interest him. I tried to make the story as succinct as possible, and I had only spoken for a minute before he stopped me.

"Aha! There's your reason, right there."

"What? Which part of it?"

"You said that Winston and his men dragged Marcelo from his horse, overpowered him, and immediately tied him up with rope."

"Yeessss." I wasn't catching on. Why would that keep Marcelo from doing magic?

"After the men tied Marcelo, he didn't even try to do magic, did he?"

"No, I suppose he didn't."

"Well, there you go."

I sighed. He was going to make me ask. "And why does any of this prevent Marcelo from doing magic?"

"Ah, I've been a magician for so long that sometimes I

forget what the novice doesn't yet know. Marcelo couldn't do magic once your attackers bound him with the rope. He knew that so he didn't even try."

"And why couldn't he do magic because he was tied?" I hoped I wasn't coming off as dense, but I just wasn't getting it.

"My dear, it's impossible for a magician to do magic when he—or she—is tied. We've all tried many times before, as an exercise, but there's no way around it. The act of binding physically also binds the magician's power. We aren't sure why exactly, or how this began, but it's the way it's been for as long as we remember."

I finally understood why Marcelo had done nothing to defend us, and why it had been me, the initiate who couldn't control her powers, that saved us.

"This limitation has caused countless witches and wizards to suffer. The ignorant townspeople are too cowardly to attack magicians alone, so they congregate in mobs to do their dirty work. If they manage to surprise the magicians, they can often knock them unconscious before the witch or wizard has the chance to react. Once the magicians are unconscious, the mob restrains them, effectively *binding* their magic as well as their bodies. By the time the magicians wake, they're incapable of doing magic, and they've usually been tied to a pyre.

"The magician dies a terrible, excruciating death by fire. Whenever our kind is present to witness a burning, we use magic to remove the victim's pain."

"Why not just save the witch then?" I asked. Why allow the witch to suffer death at all?

"Because it must be this way—for now. If we were to reveal how truly powerful we are, we would be persecuted endlessly. But there may soon come a time when that will change. For many centuries, we've been waiting for the right one to come and lead us into an age of enlightenment."

Did he mean his kind had been waiting for centuries? Or did he actually mean he and his brother had been alive and waiting for centuries?

"The courageous magicians who've died at the stake have all taken our secrets with them to the grave, often through unbearable pain, because they understood how important it was that they do so. Imagine if everybody knew how powerful we really are? And then imagine if they realized all they had to do was tie us up? Then they could kill us off easily. But as long as our kind preserves its secrets, we'll continue."

The old man narrowed his eyes at me. "You can't tell this to anyone."

I startled. His tone of voice had turned violent, and he directed that aggression at me. It was as if he suddenly suspected I would betray his entire kind to a terrible death. I blinked up at him, frightened.

"No one can ever know," he hissed.

I nodded silently, overwhelmed by the sudden change in this man. Marcelo had warned me the brothers were difficult to deal with, but he hadn't given me reason to be scared of them.

Albacus continued in a fierce voice, as if the ferocity of how he said what he said would force me to comply. It occurred to me that maybe it would.

"You can never tell another living soul. Our kind has survived for thousands of years because no one who intends to harm us has discovered this one weakness. We hide our weaknesses, and they are few. The repercussions will be swift and severe if you were to betray us."

He bore down on me with bulging eyes. Taller than me, he seemed to tower over me now more than he had before.

I gulped and managed to squeak out a response. "I won't tell anyone. I promise."

And just like that, he backed down.

"Good," he said, in his normal voice. "You now have a duty to protect our kind."

He said this casually, but I wanted to blurt out: Why? Why did I have all this responsibility I hadn't asked for? I had no intention to betray anybody, especially unnecessarily, but why was this now my duty?

"We're all in this together in the end. In a peculiar chain of necessity created by factors such as this secret, the seasoned magician depends on the novice for his safety as much as the novice depends on the practiced magician for guidance and protection. Our kind depends on one another.

"You've now become a link in this chain," he added, as if it were an obvious conclusion, and I suppose that it was.

"And you know that saying, 'A chain is only as strong as its weakest link?' Well, this is especially applicable to our kind."

"*Our* kind?" I asked, before I could stop myself.

I wasn't sure if I was ready to hear his answer. Because, in the end, I knew it before he even confirmed it. There were some things I suppose every witch knows somewhere deep down before anyone tells her.

It was one thing to consider myself capable of magic—perhaps, *just perhaps*, a witch even—but it was quite another to consider myself inextricably entangled to a magical world, *a kind*, I knew nothing about. I didn't think I was ready to be a link in a chain that bound me to an underworld fraught with danger and mystery. I wasn't ready to be one of Albacus' *kind*.

Albacus snapped his head back in laughter. It was not lost on me that it had only been a minute since he'd been vicious toward me. I was clearly unable to predict the man's emotional responses.

"Yes, my child, *our* kind."

This time I was certain. His tone of voice was mocking.

"You hover up the steepest mountain around on air, carrying horses, carts, and men, doing magic out in the open without a worry in the world"—I thought that was unfair; I was very worried, doing it all to save Marcelo —"and you wonder whether you are one of *our* kind? Without a doubt in the world, child, you're a witch. A magician. One of *our* kind. Do you understand now?"

I couldn't decide whether to be angry at his derisiveness, shocked by what I already knew, or one of the other many emotions that coursed through me now. *Me, a witch? A real witch? One of a magical kind that had existed for much longer than I knew, with powers I could not yet fathom?* Until I met Marcelo, it had never occurred to me, not even as a remote possibility.

"If I'm a witch, why couldn't I do magic before I met Marcelo?"

Albacus studied me with a curious look on his face.

"Did you ever try to do magic before you met Marcelo?" he asked.

I shook my head. Of course I hadn't. Why would I? It was the furthest thing from my mind. Mother and Father had taught me that magic was a wicked thing.

"You may have always been able to do magic. But it's equally possible that it hasn't come about until now because the magic was waiting for you to go through puberty, to see how you emerged. We may never find out. There are times, though they're rare, when the magic waits to see whether a host of this incredible skill will be receptive to it and whether the required structure has come together to properly support it. You're... sixteen? Seventeen?"

"I'll be seventeen soon, on the spring equinox."

"Really? That's fascinating."

But Albacus didn't say what was fascinating. He seemed to be examining my physical appearance. I reached my hand up to smooth my hair. Within moments, I brought it back down. The effort would be futile. My hair was tangled in offshoots all around my head. Again I thought I must look like Medusa with red snakes slithering around her like a halo. Perhaps there was a painting of this very frightening image in the brothers' ancestral dark art collection.

I had already come to realize how frustrating conversations with Albacus were. For every question of mine he answered, I discovered two more I wanted to ask. I hoped he had the patience to answer them all.

I wouldn't receive an answer to the next question I intended to ask, but I would discover that patience was not Albacus' forte.

"Enough questions for today."

Without another word, he turned and started to walk away, down the dark entry hall farther into the castle.

I hesitated for only a moment, but then seized it before it passed. "What should I do now?" I called after him.

"What you do now and for the rest of today is your business. Tomorrow, what you do becomes my business."

What did that mean? It was exasperating.

"Do I stay in the castle then? Will I sleep here?"

"Where else would you go? Tomorrow we begin training. You'll need all your strength for training," he said without breaking stride. His voice was becoming more faint with the distance he put between us.

"Training for what?"

"For who you are meant to become." Then he turned a corner and disappeared.

I wrapped my coat more tightly around me and looked into the dark, silent stone that surrounded me on all sides. I stood alone, in a castle with three magicians I barely knew, far away from everything that was familiar to me.

But somehow, despite all my confusion and discomfort, I knew I was exactly where I was supposed to be.

(New adult space fantasy)

Planet Origins

Original Elements

Holographic Princess

Purple Worlds

Planet Sand

Holographic Convergence

Mowab Rider

THE LIGHT WARRIORS

(Visionary fantasy - a complete series)

Beyond Sedona

Beyond Prophecy

Beyond Amber

Beyond Arnaka

DRAGON FORCE

(Young adult space fantasy - a complete series)

Invisible Born *

Invisible Bound *

Invisible Rider *

POCKET PORTALS

(Young adult paranormal fantasy)

The Orphan Son *

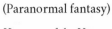

(Paranormal fantasy)
Huntress of the Unseen

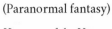

(Time travel romance)
A Betrayal of Time

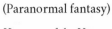

(Magical realism)
Daughter of the Wind

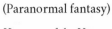

(Superhero satire)
The Unkillable Killer

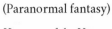

(Magical realism)
Whispers of Pachamama

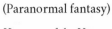

(Science fiction)
Immortalium *

(* coming soon)

For an updated list of Lucía's books, please visit her website:
www.LuciaAshta.com.

ABOUT THE AUTHOR

Lucía Ashta, a former attorney and architect, is an Argentinian-American author who lives in Sedona with her beloved and three daughters. She published her first story (about an unusual Cockatoo) at the age of eight, and she's been at it ever since.

Learn about Lucía's books at LuciaAshta.com.